720 Heartbeats

JAKA TOMC

Neja, to be with you is a dream come true.
I love you.

CHAPTER ONE

Fourteen minutes. Fourteen fucking minutes to go and there is nothing I can do. And God knows I tried, I really did. I did everything in my power to prevent it. I feel so small. Insignificant. A speck of dust in this vast mysterious Universe. I am going to lose the love of my life, and I am just sitting here, downing a bottle of Jameson, trying to keep my tears from flowing. I am about to end my pathetic life with my service Glock. I can not and do not want to live without her.

Twelve minutes to go. Seven hundred and twenty heartbeats. I will have to make the most of them. But will this change anything? No. Life is not a fairy-tale. There are no happy endings. That is just some bullshit that the movie industry tries to sell us. An illusion of reality. All stories end in tears. I would like to crack open the skull of the jackass who said that every new beginning is disguised as a painful ending, and eat his fucking pea-sized brain. Ten minutes. One hundred breaths.

I took my Swiss Army knife from the suitcase, opened up the blade and tested its tip with my finger. I placed my left hand on the table and shoved the knife through it, using my right hand. No hesitation, whatsoever. The small knife dug itself into the wood. There was hardly any blood. No pain. As I was looking at the red handle of the blade that had pierced my palm, I felt a tingling sensation in my index finger.

CHAPTER TWO

Monday morning. Five-fifteen. I drove past the bakery and saw Kemal loading fresh buns into a white van with a large orange and black sign on its side. Every time I saw him I remembered the night his first son, Kerim, was born, about three years ago. We got completely wasted, but nobody expected us to break into a basketball arena, strip naked and play a game of five on five. It was not about winning it, it was about having a great time. Well, at least until Speedy hit the floor and nearly tore his dick off. His wife Sandra was not pleased with the total lack of interest nor the performance in bed over the next three weeks. Nevertheless, the night was unforgettable. It was one of those nights that buries itself deep inside your cerebral cortex and remains there forever. A night of true happiness. A moment that you want to freeze and preserve for eternity.

I parked in front of the headquarters, turned off the engine, waited for the song on the radio to end and slowly stepped out of the car. Boris was standing outside the building with two cups of coffee in one hand and a cigarette in the other. He waved in my direction and then continued talking to Tina. She truly was one of a kind. She decided to become a detective at the age of twenty-three. Until then she had worked in a strip club, where she had a single rule – never sleep with a client. The local Casanova once decided it would be fun to shove a finger up her pussy. She broke his hand in three places. She knew how

2

to take care of herself better than most men and that was something I really admired about her. Seeing as I have never been to her club, I was not subjected to her rule and this led to a couple of wonderful weeks just before I met Sara.

"Good morning, Rok," she greeted me with her soft voice.

Boris merely nodded and pushed the cup of coffee into my hand.

"It's fucking freezing today. It doesn't feel like spring, does it?" I murmured.

Over the past few days the temperatures had plummeted by more than ten degrees and even though it was almost the end of March, we had to take our warm winter clothes back out from the closets. Tina looked at me with her deep blue eyes and smiled. She still regretted our story ending. It was written all over her face every time we bumped into each other. Of course this happened almost every day. However, she never gave me the desperate 'why are you with her and not me' look. It was an honest, pleasant, tender look. I liked her, but everything changed the moment Sara stepped into my life. She was the one I had been waiting for. I knew she was special the very first time I laid eyes on her. I could feel her on a different level. It felt as if we had known each other for centuries.

"What the fuck are you dreaming about now?" mumbled Boris. "Let's get to work. Horvat wants us to solve the bloody Fire Dawn case today. I need you to remain focused, do you understand?! I took a bullet for you once, and I don't want to save your sorry ass again today."

I smiled.

"Don't worry you stupid old fart. Today is our day."

Tina remained silent, but her deep blue eyes spoke volumes.

CHAPTER THREE

"Man, I'm going ballistic. Milena hasn't put out for nine straight days in a row. She says I only pay attention to her when my dick is in her mouth. Can you imagine?! That I don't take notice. Apparently, I never tell her that I love her. Can you fucking believe it?"

I was gazing through the window, watching children play in the park nearby. A little boy in a bright red parka was chasing two girls who were trying to run away, screaming at the top of their lungs. I remembered how carefree we used to be when we were kids. We would not have known a problem if it sneaked up to us and bit us in the face. No expectations and no disappointments. We merely lived pure lives. Unspoiled by the past and with no cares about the future.

"Yesterday I wanted to call Barbara, take her out for dinner and then fuck her on the backseat of my Volvo. I'm serious, I no longer give a fuck. Women are holding us by the balls and I don't want to take it anymore. Hey, are you listening to me?!"

I looked at him and nodded.

"No matter what you do, women will always have the last word. There's nothing you can do about it. Yes, they're holding us by the balls, but we love them for it," I explained.

"What the fuck? Have you switched sides or something? Man up and tell me what you think. What you really think. This is no laughing matter, Rok."

When something stuck in Boris's head there was no way you could persuade him to look at it from a different angle.

"Listen, I'm not taking sides here. I'm only telling you how I see it. The moment you fall in love with a woman, the moment you give her your heart, your fate is sealed. From that moment on, she's the one pulling all the strings in your life. She becomes the puppeteer. The real question is why we allow ourselves to be led. Whether we admit it or not, we seem to like it. Do you remember the photograph of a little boy looking down a little girl's panties? She's saying: 'I will use this to control your life'. Well, that's how it is. You better accept it."

Boris was silently staring through the windscreen. But he did not stay silent for long.

"I'm sure Sara and you don't have these problems. I advise you to never get married. You're doomed the moment you put a ring on her finger. It's the end, the abso-fucking-lute end. Your fate is sealed. You become a toy in her hands. Screw a life like that!"

I nudged him with my elbow. "I think it's started."

Kolya was a well-known dealer. We had been pursuing him for quite a while, but he always managed to slip through our net somehow. We had arrested him twice, but never managed to pin anything on him. He was a clever little bastard. He had connections everywhere, even in our department. But Kolya was a small-time crook. We were not really interested in him. We were only going after him because we thought he might lead us to Walter. He was our real target. He was also impossible to find. The man was an enigma, a ghost that moved undetected in the belly of society. We did not have a single photograph of him or an address. In fact, we had absolutely nothing on him. The only thing we knew was that he was forty years old, give or take a few summers. He had constructed a sound hierarchal system so that no one he did not trust with his life could reach him directly. In fact, only two people could: Zoran, also known as The Accountant, and Brane, also known as Scout. Kolya was second in line, taking instructions directly from The Accountant. He was in charge of the cocaine route between Trieste and central Slovenia, but as he was not a dealer, he never had any drugs on him. The small dealers never got drugs directly from him, but through intermediaries, called 'carts'. Kolya handled sixty kilograms of Columbian cocaine each month. He took ten percent of the money, which meant he earned approximately two hundred thousand euros a month. He has wasted three-quarters of his money on classy hookers, expensive champagne and luxury cars. I know it sounds like a stereotype, but that is how things are in life.

"Look at that dickhead. He's going in," hollered Boris.

The plan was simple. Kolya has arranged a meeting with Mehmed Zarifović, aka The Blacksmith. They were planning a new drug route through Rijeka. They were discussing Violet Storm, a new synthetic drug that amplified the synaptic transmissions in the brain by three hundred percent. It had a very short lasting effect, only about fifteen minutes, but the demand was enormous, regardless of its price, making it inaccessible to mere mortals. The cost? Five hundred euros per pill.

"Two minutes to intervention," said chief inspector Horvat over the radio.

I took my gun, unlocked its safety catch and returned it to its holster.

"Rock 'n' roll," I said, my heart beating madly like it always did before we jumped into action.

"Man, my balls are so blue, I can hardly sit down," croaked Boris.

How can he possibly be thinking about his balls at a

moment like this, I thought.

* * *

"Everybody hit the floor!" I yelled, waving my gun from side to side. I knew Kolya was unarmed, but he was always surrounded by three armed bodyguards. I jumped on the first one. As he took a swing at me, I ducked and punched him in his solar plexus. As he was trying to catch his breath, I swiftly moved behind his back and kicked him in the back of the knee. As he keeled over, I grabbed him by the neck and held him in a chokehold until he fainted.

"Don't do anything stupid," yelled Boris while pressing the second bodyguard against the floor, trying to disarm him with his free hand.

"You fucking police cunts, a man can't even enjoy his lunch in peace!" yelled Kolya as Horvat pushed his knee into his ribs.

"I'll sue you for police brutality, you fucking pigs!"

I looked around the place. Everything was under control. The operation was a success. Kolya will not get away this time. We managed to do what we set out to do and at the end of the day, that is what matters. Day after day. Successes and failures.

CHAPTER FOUR

She kissed me passionately and sincerely like always. She was undoubtedly the most sincere person I have met in my thirty-two years of life. Besides my mum, of course. Sara was the closest I could find to a soul mate. Not so much because we were similar, but because we completed each other. Every moment I spent with her was an opportunity to grow and learn. I have learned so much during the seven months I have known her and I know that she has molded me into a better man. She has opened my eyes and, more importantly, she has opened my heart. I can be myself when I am with her. It was only after we got together that I became aware of how insincere my previous escapades were. Sara never judged me. She always listened to me, considered what I told her and then gave me her opinion. She had a unique way of sharing her thoughts, views, and opinions. It was as if everything that came out of her beautiful mouth was the absolute truth. She was a true wordsmith, which was hardly surprising, seeing as she had been working in PR for the past five years.

"Milena told me she and Boris are having problems," she said almost as soon as we sat down.

"I know, he mentioned it," I replied.

"I totally understand her. Boris can be a selfish bastard. Did you know he hasn't gone down on her in two months?!"

I was putting lasagna on my plate.

"No, he failed to mention that," I said.

"Well I think that's just plain selfish and there's no room for selfishness in a serious and honest relationship."

I nodded. I was as hungry as a wolf so I stuck the fork into the deliciously steamy pile of food in front of me.

"If you tried to pull off something like that, I'd teach you a lesson," she said as she underlined her statement with a slightly mischievous look.

"Don't worry, he'll get back into it. He won't last a week without dipping it in. He will succumb, I know him."

Fuck, she makes one hell of a lasagna.

"This is the problem. Men only change when women push them up against a wall. Unfortunately, you usually don't change for long and shortly after it's all back to how it used to be. You should come to these conclusions on your own. Don't you think all parties involved should enjoy sex?"

She sat down and started eating.

"And while we're on the subject, I want to feel you inside me. Right here, on this table. Right now!"

I looked at her, holding a piece of lasagna in front of my mouth and a hard-on between my legs.

* * *

"This is what I'm talking about. Spontaneous moments. Sex, the moment you think of it."

She inhaled and passed the joint to me. The sky was unusually starry, not a cloud in sight. We were sitting on the terrace, hugging, and discussing all sorts of things like we did on most evenings. I cherished these moments. I adored her as she wholeheartedly defended her opinions, but always left some room to include yours. That is if the arguments persuaded her. I love her. I love her like I have never loved anyone before.

"Can you bring me another glass of Jameson?" she asked with her soft voice.

"Of course," I replied as I went to the kitchen.

I started reminiscing about the first evening we met in a bar called Daktari. I expected her to order a glass of wine or a mojito. That is what I would expect from a sophisticated woman. Judging by what I saw at first glance, it did not occur to me to think of her being anything less than cosmopolitan. She ordered a double Jameson on the rocks. I fell for her that very second. The next few days and weeks offered thousands of similar surprises, all of which I adored. I took the bottle from the fridge, threw three ice cubes into the glass and poured three fingers of whiskey over them. Sara could hold her liquor better than most men, and I found that utterly fascinating. One night, we got seriously drunk. I was seeing double and considering spilling my guts all over the terrace while she appeared entirely sober. I have no idea how she does it. I passed the glass to her. A warm smile appeared on her luscious lips. A smile that could thaw the coldest of hearts. God, how I love this woman.

CHAPTER FIVE

"I'd rather die this very second than roll my own cigarettes," said Boris.

I did not agree. Until recently, I had smoked only hand-rolled cigarettes. They helped me smoke less and the rolling calmed me down. Smoking a cigarette that you have rolled yourself was completely different to smoking one that came from a conveyor belt and was identical to a billion other cigarettes. However, I recently started buying ready-made smokes. I have no idea why. Maybe because I like the illusion of having a choice. When the last Marlboro man died, Boris switched to Luckies. He was a man of principle.

"What's new with Milena?" I asked.

"You won't believe it, but she started attending some sort of a book club. She spends all her evenings there."

"At least that gives you some peace and quiet."

"Fuck peace. I've been forced to make my own dinner three nights in a row. And as you're familiar with my cooking skills, you know that I haven't been going to bed a happy man."

"Let her be. You're only encouraging her by letting her know that you are bothered by what she does."

"Hmm. You might be right. I'm telling you, it's unbearable. I've had enough of this shit!"

"You'd better face it. This is what married life is all about. You need to compromise."

He had brought me to our street. It was an average day. Most of the day was spent doing paperwork. Somewhere in between, we went for a spin through town, but nothing unusual happened.

"Say hello to Sara for me," he said as he sped off.

"Is everything okay?" she asked me as I stepped into the living room.

"Yes, it was a rather mundane day," I responded. "What's in that packet?"

I pointed to a medium sized packet in the middle of the coffee table.

"I have no idea. It's addressed to you. It doesn't say who sent it and the postman didn't have a clue. Open it and we'll see."

I grabbed the packet and inspected it with my trained eye. The paper seemed old. I had never seen anything like it. The packet had no distinguishing marks, no address, nothing.

"What do you think is in it?"

"I have no idea, honey. Open it."

I lifted it. It was quite heavy. I shook it, looking for something suspicious. I could not hear anything.

"Surely it's not …"

I started tearing off the paper. Underneath the first layer was another layer of paper, this one burgundy red. Strange. I tore this one off too. Underneath the red paper there was a black laptop.

"Does this seem familiar to you?" I asked Sara and pushed the contents of the packet towards her. She took it into her hands and took a closer look.

"Isn't this your laptop? The one that was stolen."

"It certainly is," I replied.

I took it from Sara's hands, placed it on the table, opened it and turned it on. About thirty seconds later I was looking at a very familiar desktop.

"It's mine, that's for sure," I said to Sara, checking the icons on the desktop.

Something wasn't right. Everything was the way I left it except for a new icon: a Word file that was entitled 'Diary'. I clicked on the icon and a short document appeared on the screen. I started reading.

March 25, 2015, 4:45 a.m.
The morning was just like any other. I made my coffee and took it to the terrace, where I smoked my first cigarette of the day and watched the world waking up. I love mornings. Everything is so peaceful and primal. I'm a blank canvas. No thoughts, no feelings, only me, my cup of coffee and my cigarette. I would like to write a book one day, but I have no idea how to start. Well, I know, I just don't take the time to actually do it. What if this is going to be the beginning of my book? Enough daydreaming, I need to get dressed …

Who would write a diary on my computer? Well, to be precise, the beginning of a diary seeing as the short paragraph was all that was written. But something stood out. The date. It was March 24 today.

"Sara, this is weird!"
"What is it, darling?"
"My desktop has a new file entitled Diary and the document only has a few sentences in it, but it all starts tomorrow. Take a look."
Sara stood next to me and read the document.
"Interesting."
"It's weird, isn't it?"
"It really is unusual."

I took the laptop into my hands, turned it around and searched for any trace that might reveal the identity of the perpetrator. I failed to find anything out of the ordinary. What sort of a fool would steal my computer, write a few of his morning thoughts on it – very obviously get the date wrong - save the document to the desktop and then send the computer back to me. I re-read the text again. I had a funny feeling that I knew the writer. The flow of his words was extremely familiar. I realized that this mystery would not get solved tonight, so I shut down the laptop and went to the kitchen for another glass of wine. Tomorrow is a new day, I thought. Who knows what revelations it will bring.

* * *

I woke up just before five, made myself some coffee and lit the first cigarette of the day on the terrace. I enjoy the tranquility of the morning. I wake up with nature and this fills me with the energy I need to get me through my daily routine. Life is made up of moments and we have to focus on the ones that fulfill us. Unfortunately, most people do the exact opposite. They focus their time and energy on negative thoughts that lead to negative actions. They fall into a vicious cycle of negativity. Escape is nearly impossible. An avalanche of lies, deceit and hypocrisy overtakes them. First, they lie to others, then they lie to themselves. If they are lucky, they will look into the mirror one day and admit that they can not go on like this. If they are unlucky, they will fail. Life is a fucking lottery. There is only a handful of lucky winners. Most folks just hand over their change week after week, hoping that Lady Luck will visit them one day. A benevolent force that is believed to be an unbiased embodiment of a feminine universal do-gooder, who grants good fortune to those in need. People who are caught in the clutches of modern-day liberalism. Superstitious fucks. Welcome to planet Earth.

CHAPTER SIX

Some people do not like surprises. I am not one of
them. I have always loved those thrilling sources of
amazement. They awaken the primal, childish and
innocent side of me. Of course, they can be of varying
intensities. On one side of the spectrum, there are the
almost expected surprises. But even these can catch you
off guard. On the other hand, there are those that knock
your socks off and keep you gaping with your mouth wide
open. However, there is also a third category of surprises –
surprises so shocking that you have to pinch yourself to
make sure you are not dreaming.

March 26, 2015, 6.25 p.m.
I still can't get my mind around what had happened. I've never
felt anything like this in my life. Such a rush of anger, animal rage, a
desire for revenge. As I sat in the car parked in front of the hospital,
I wanted to drive through town and kill the bastard who shot him. I
held back. Not because it would have been bad for my career, but
because I broke down and cried like a baby the very next moment.
The anger built up and was transformed into an unbearable sadness
that poured out of me. It could have been me. It should have been me.

I closed the laptop and sat on the sofa with my mouth
wide open. What had just happened? What did I just read?
Who wrote this? How did a new entry appear in the diary?
Who was trying to make a fool out of me?

"Sara, did anybody stop by today?"

"No. Why?"

"I think somebody's messing with me. Look at this."

I pushed the laptop under her nose. She read the entry.

"Is this the same document?"

"Yes. But I don't get it. I can't believe it's writing itself."

"And again it has tomorrow's date. Somebody's obviously hacked your computer and is screwing with you."

"What? Who?"

"I don't know. Somebody. People do this sort of stuff. But I'm not the one with a shiny badge."

"I'll take it to our forensic lab tomorrow. They'll track down the bastard."

"That'd probably be for the best."

Surprises ensure that our lives momentarily shift from the predictable tracks, which we have grown accustomed to and live by, to the unknown unpredictable tracks that simultaneously bestow joy and a hint of fear upon us. We would become slaves of our own self-control if it were not for surprises. It is strange that we want to control something that has not happened yet. But it is equally strange that we have a desire to deal with the past, even though we can no longer change it. In our heads, we roam amidst past events and all of the various potential scenarios in the more or less distant future. Nobody knows what will happen in the future, but we want to be prepared for as many events as possible. We are like chess players, trying to predict the opponent's future moves, but in this case, we are dealing with life itself. True masters do not play the game on a single chessboard, but on multiple chessboards at the same time. And what is the difference between grandmasters and masters? Surprise. Moves that cannot be predicted by an opponent. Life can play a game of chess with seven billion people at the same time and it can take each and every one of us by surprise. And yet we still believe we are capable of winning because we can predict three or four moves to come. We are insignificant. Our pathetic attempts to play the game of life and death all end in the same way. It does not even matter how good of a player you were. When your times comes, you lose it all. Life's final surprise.

CHAPTER SEVEN

It was five minutes to five in the morning and I was pulling on my blue boxers. I kissed Sara and she let out a mumble that was barely audible. I watched her for a few moments, before I closed the bedroom door, took the keys and left the house. I drove to the headquarters and parked the car. I could not see Boris anywhere, but that was not unusual – he was sick all the time. He was like a little schoolboy trying to skip school. If you were seeing him for the first time, you would never suspect that such a robust man could be knocked out of action and into bed by the smallest of colds.

Tina was standing outside, by herself, smoking a cigarette and sipping tea. She hugged me, which was slightly unusual, but I also noticed that her eyes were puffy and full of tears. I asked her what was wrong. She was quiet for a while and then she finally uttered: "Boris," and burst into tears. That was worrying, so I asked her what has happened to Boris. She sniffled twice and told me he had been shot and was lying in the hospital. Both, Milena and Boris had been shot. In the middle of the night, in their own house. I looked at her in disbelief, grabbed her by her shoulders, shook her and demanded that she tell me more.

"Milena is dead," she said as she burst into tears again. "Boris is in a critical condition. The doctors say he'll be lucky to live to see another day."

I stared at the wall. What a fucked up situation. But Boris was as tough as nails and if anyone could survive this, it had to be him. All of our conversations about our fleeting existence flashed in front of my eyes. It was during those conversations that I usually told Boris, who was always eager to point out that death is just around the corner, that he would outlive us all. At the age of thirty-one he was way too young to be meeting his maker.

Tina calmed down enough to tell me Horvat wanted to see me and that he was waiting in his office. I left her alone. She was in shock, the poor thing. I entered the building and walked towards Horvat's office. The atmosphere was bleak; everybody was silently staring at their screens. It was the exact opposite of a regular day. I did not like it at all. I could hear Horvat long before I entered the office. I knew he suspected someone, but he did not seem ready to share that information with me just yet. He said it was too dangerous seeing as Boris was my partner and he did not want to take any risks. He told me Boris was in the hospital, in a coma, and he suggested I take some time off to visit him.

"Take tomorrow off too, take some time for yourself," he said as I was leaving his office.

The hospital was no more than a few minutes' drive from headquarters. My hands were trembling. Boris was my best friend. To be honest, he was my only real friend. I took my cell phone from my pocket and called Sara. I told her what had happened and she broke down and cried. I was powerless on the other side of the line, and all that I could do was listen to her weep and imagine the tears that she was shedding in that brief moment when time and the world around us seemed to stand still. As I said goodbye I brought the car to a halt, about a hundred meters from the hospital's entrance. I turned the engine off and stared into the distance. I wanted revenge. I had the urge to drive to a few particular addresses and visit some people who knew what was going on in Ljubljana underground scene. As soon as I would find out the name of the son of a bitch who shot my partner and murdered his wife, I would track him down, stick the barrel of my gun down his throat and empty the entire clip. I did not care about anything. An eye for an eye. A life for a life. My plans went right out the window the moment I broke down and started crying. I had not wept like this since I was thirteen and my dog Kiki died. Tears rolled down my cheeks and washed away my thirst for blood.

* * *

I stood next to the hospital bed, staring at my best friend. I had never seen him so serene. He was on life support. The doctors had hooked him up to a ventilator that helped him with his breathing. I will kill the scumbag who did this. It was the only thought that went through my mind. For a moment, I thought I saw Boris move, but I realized my imagination was running wild. These fantasies were being fed by my desire to see my buddy sit up straight again while he would give me crap about the tears that were running down my face. No, he was still lying motionless in front of me.

"Don't give up, old friend," I said to him. "Don't abandon me."

"Are you okay, sweetie?" a soft angelic voice came from behind my back.

Sara was standing in the doorway. I moved towards her with gentle strides and hugged her with such strength that I almost cracked her ribs.

"How is he?"

"The doctor said that the next two days will be critical. He's in a coma. He has a ruptured spleen and his right lung wing has been pierced by a bullet."

"Oh my God," said Sara, as her eyes filled up with

tears.

"We have to stay strong, for his sake."

"Why has this happened? Who would do something like this?"

"I'm almost certain that it was organized by Walter or one of his men. Given that this happened two days after Kolya's been arrested, I'd dare to say that it would be too big of a coincidence if they had nothing to do with it at all."

"Who? Who are these people?"

"They're bad people, sweetheart. But there's no need for you to worry about them."

"How can I not worry? They shot our best friends! What if we're next?"

"I'll do everything in my power to make sure we're not."

The phone rang. It was Tina.

"Hi."

"How is he?"

"We'll know more in two days' time. He's still in a coma and on life support for now."

"I'll visit him after work."

"Okay."

I turned off the phone and put it back into my pocket.

"Are you up for lunch?" I asked Sara.

"Sure. But I have to be back in the office by two."

"That leaves us with plenty of time. Should we go to Jurman?"

"Okay. Sounds great to me."

* * *

"I'm telling you. Something unusual is happening."

"I can't believe it. How can a diary predict the future?"

"I have no idea, but I'm going to find out."

"Is it possible that the people you mentioned in the hospital are behind this? Maybe this is their way of telling you what's going to happen."

"I've considered that as a possibility."

"What are you going to do?"

"I'll continue as planned. I'll take my computer to the forensic lab, and I'm convinced they'll find something we've overlooked."

The waiter brought a large pizza for me and a tuna salad for Sara. I was not hungry, but I knew that I had to calm down. Adrenalin was flowing through my blood but a hearty meal could help me unwind a bit. I will have to carefully consider my next move. But most of all, I will have to remain calm and composed for Boris, for Sara and for myself.

* * *

I parked the car in front of the house and walked to the Daktari Bar. I did not feel like being alone. I sat at the bar and ordered a draught beer. Lea, the waitress, soon joined me. She had just finished her shift.

"Hi, Rok, how are you?"

"Lousy."

"What's wrong?"

"Things are messed up."

"You haven't fallen out with Sara, have you?"

"No, everything is fine with Sara. It's Boris. He's been shot and I've got no idea who did it."

"What?! For Christ's sake! Did he survive?"

"He's alive. But he's in a really bad shape."

I took a long sip of beer.

"I'll keep my fingers crossed that he pulls through."

"Thanks."

I grabbed a fistful of peanuts and chucked them into my mouth.

* * *

Three hours later I was back home. I threw myself onto the sofa and stared at the laptop on the table in front of me. I opened it and checked the Word document. There was nothing new. I will take it to the lab tomorrow, and ask them to analyze it thoroughly. They will find out who is playing these games with me. I walked triumphantly to the liquor cabinet, grabbed a bottle of Glenmorangie and poured it into a crystal glass. I smelled it and flinched. Everything would become clear tomorrow.

"Rok, have you seen this?"
Sara's voice brought me back from my daydreams.
"What?"
"There's a new entry."
In three quick steps I was standing beside her.
"Let me see."

March 27, 2015, 6:45 a.m.
I woke up in the middle of the night, drenched in sweat. Just before I woke up, I was dreaming that I opened my eyes and I was staring down the barrel of a gun. The next moment it fired and my head was blown to pieces. I looked at the time – 3:43. I got up, went to the kitchen and poured myself a glass of water. I couldn't have gone back to sleep if I wanted to, so I boiled some water for coffee and had a shower. As I drank my morning coffee, I was thinking about Boris. I was convinced he would pull through. I know he's a tough son of a bitch. He had to pull through. I got dressed and went for a walk. It is hard to describe the tranquility of the early mornings in Prule. When I got home, Sara was already up. She said she couldn't sleep anymore because she had a nightmare and was worried about Boris. She made scrambled eggs for breakfast, but I couldn't eat. I just sat there watching her. She looked gorgeous in my T-shirt and her panties as she moved around the kitchen like a cat. I stepped up to her and kissed her on the back of her neck. She hugged me and we stood motionless for a while.

"I love you," I said. She smiled at me and drew closer. I love mornings like this.

"Rok, who's behind this?"

"I don't get it. Ten minutes ago, there was no entry. I opened the document, placed the laptop onto the table, walked to the study and then I heard your voice."

"What the hell is going on?"

"Somebody must've hacked my computer just like you implied yesterday."

"And he or she is writing tomorrow's diary? That's impossible."

"I know."

"Then stop being so fucking calm!"

"You know me, always calm."

"Please take it to the forensics lab first thing in the morning. I'm scared."

"Take it easy Sara. Everything will be all right."

She stepped closer to me and tightly wrapped her hands around me. Everything will be all right, I thought. But my gut feeling was telling me something else entirely.

CHAPTER EIGHT

Life happens when you least expect it. You can prepare yourself for all possible scenarios, but it will still come hurtling towards you when you look away and there is nothing you can do about it. I was thinking about this during my early morning walk through the streets of Ljubljana. I woke up at 3:43, just as it said in the diary. I had a nightmare, precisely like the one described in the diary. I knew Sara would be up when I got home. She was making breakfast, but instead of scrambled eggs, she was preparing cereal with fruit and yogurt. It seems that the diary is not hundred percent accurate. Dumbass, of course things can change if you know what is happening in advance, I quickly reminded myself.

"You had trouble sleeping too?" I asked Sara as I took off my shoes.
"Yes, I had a nightmare."
"I see that you didn't make scrambled eggs."
"What's terrifying is that I wanted to make them, but then I remembered the diary and I changed my mind."
"I'm not hungry anyway," I responded, walked over to the table in the living room and picked up the laptop.
"There's nothing new, I've already checked."

Until now, the entries have been appearing regularly. A new entry would appear around six in the afternoon and it would always describe the following day. But what really worried me was that the diary was written by somebody who not only thinks like me but also forms sentences like me. The only logical explanation that I could come up with was that I was writing these entries. But how?

"Sara, have you noticed anything unusual in the diary?"

"You mean except for the fact that it predicts the future?"

"Yes, except for that."

"It's written as if it was written by you. It must be written by somebody who knows you well, somebody who is familiar with your habits and your way of thinking."

"Exactly. This person is writing the exact same way as I would've written it. He uses the same vocabulary, the same word order. It's as if he thinks the same way I do. Sara, I must be the one writing these entries."

She smiled and gave me a strange look. "You're talking nonsense, sweetie. That's impossible."

"I know."

"So how do you think this happens?"

"I haven't got a clue. Maybe my future self is writing to my present self. Do you think that might be possible?"

"I think you've read too much science fiction. I think somebody is playing a prank on us. You need to take your computer to forensics as soon as possible. I'm sure that they'll discover who's behind this sick joke."

Sara. She was always my voice of reason. However, in this case, the reason failed. Even if somebody was writing the diary as me, it is impossible to guess and predict things that have not happened yet. I could not decide what was harder to believe. That the diary was writing itself or that it was written by someone who knew me too well and had the ability to predict the future. Or that it was me writing it at some point in the future. I had three possible scenarios and all of them were highly improbable. Unbelievable even. But Sara was right; no matter what they will discover in the forensic lab, it will always trump the lack of intel we have now.

* * *

As indicated by its name, the forensic laboratory is primarily a laboratory. The employees in this facility research the tangible traces that are left behind on crime scenes by the perpetrators. Consequently, after carefully examining the evidence, they will offer their interpretation of the results to the police and judicial bodies. They can work their magic with these new clues afterward. Occasionally, they carry out investigations on material traces that emerge in civil legal matters. As part of its work, the Slovene National Forensic Laboratory uses over one hundred different methods to investigate an average of ten thousand cases a year. Just like on TV, forensics also perform fieldwork when necessary. In these cases, they will assist officers with the crime scene investigation and sometimes even help them with searching houses and so on. There was a time when I was really thinking about becoming a forensic expert, but given that chemistry was not my strong suit, I had to stop fantasizing about this job.

"Peter, I've brought you something," I told the head of the forensic team.

I handed him my laptop and he looked at me with a puzzled expression on his face.

"What is it?"

I put the laptop on the table, opened it and clicked on the diary.

"You wouldn't believe me if I told you. Either somebody is trying to make a fool out of me or I've stumbled across something never seen before. Whatever the case might be, I need a detailed analysis of the laptop with the emphasis on this file."

"No problem, Rok. I'll have the results by tomorrow afternoon."

"Fantastic."

I walked down the white hallway to the coffee machine, threw thirty cents into it and pressed the button. It made the whirring sound coffee machines always make and a few seconds later I had a plastic cup with a coffee-milk drink in my hands. It was not even close to the coffee I made at home, usually in a stovetop espresso maker. But people get used to anything and, in the five years I have been working at the station, I have gotten used to this coffee broth or as my co-workers called it lovingly - pussy water. I poured the pussy water with milk down my throat and walked towards the exit. It was 1:13 p.m.: hospital visiting hours.

* * *

I knew Boris was a tough cookie, but this time I did not believe he would pull through. I watched him lying motionless on the bed, connected to a ventilator. It was hard seeing him so helpless, but I could feel he was putting up an epic fight. He wanted to live. He knew his time had not come yet. He was laughing in the face of death. I wondered what the other side was like. I wanted to know whether he had gone through that famous tunnel and was drawn towards that infamous bright, white light. Is he still there?

"Don't walk towards the light," I whispered into his ear.

Not a twitch.

"Your story here isn't finished yet," I continued, convinced that he could hear me.

His heart rate went up slightly. Well, that was what the machine he was attached to showed me. The machine emitted regular beeps that informed those around him on the rhythm of his heart.

"I know you can hear me," I tried once again. "And I

know you're strong and won't give up. Fight! Can you hear me? Fight!"

Beep, beep, beep, beep. A regular, soothing rhythm with which my sleeping friend was communicating with me. A nurse walked into the room. She was tall, blond, maybe twenty-five years old.

"Hello," she greeted me.

"Hello, nurse. How is he?"

"He is stable for now, but you will need to speak to the doctor for any additional information."

"Where can I find the doctor?"

"Doctor Novak finished his rounds for today, and already went home, but he'll be back tomorrow. It's best that you come sometime after eleven, if you wish to speak to him about your friend."

She started changing the bag of saline solution.

"There you go mister Oblak, we don't want you dehydrating, do we?"

"Can he hear you?" I asked.

"I doubt it. But talking to them makes me feel better."

I nodded. The nurse smiled and left the room. I looked around. I could see a vase full of flowers standing on the table in front of me. Tall, red flowers. The only red flowers I recognized were roses and carnations, all the others were a mystery to me. I wondered where the tradition of bringing flowers to a hospital came from. I can understand bringing flowers to women. We all know they have an obsession with bright colors, aesthetics and fragrant aromas. The average man cares about flowers as much as he does about the flavor of the fruit tea he drinks when he has a cold. A brown box of chocolates was laying next to the flowers, nicely wrapped with a bow on top. I have no idea what it is like to wake up from a coma after your wife has been killed, but I imagine chocolates are not the first thing on your mind. Or are they? I sat on the chair next to the bed and started contemplating life. I realized how fragile it was. One moment you are here, full of enthusiasm, dreams, desires, and expectations. Full of ideas about the future, considering what is present and what is missing, what could have been and what will never be. You are experiencing the entire spectrum of emotions that let you know you are alive. The next moment you are dead, and all that is left is eternal darkness. In the best possible scenario, you are not aware of it, your story on this planet is brought to an end. All that remains of you is merely a memory in the mind of the loved ones who you have left behind. In the worst possible case, your soul will keep on going after death. Why is this unfortunate? Because that could prove that there is a creator, someone pulling all the strings. And I believe that this maker of ours has done an appalling job of designing the world as we know it. Hence, I cannot trust him with anything else, let alone with everlasting life after death.

Boris's arm twitched. This time I was certain it was not a figment of my imagination.

"Nurse! Quick! He moved!"

Two nurses, the tall cover girl from before and another one, also blond, but at least fifty years old, came rushing into the room.

"What happened?" asked the older nurse.

"He moved his hand."

Boris was laying there motionless. Everything was just like it was a minute ago.

"Maybe you just imagined it. Sometimes, when someone really wants something to happen ..."

"I can tell the difference between reality and fantasy, thank you very much," I interrupted her.

"There's no reason to be rude. You wouldn't believe how many times I've listened to relatives explaining how they saw their loved one move. Sometimes they've even heard their voice, whole sentences as if they were truly speaking. But none of it was true. The brain is a complex biochemical machine and our desires can be compelling."

"Thank you for this short lecture, but trust me when I tell you that Boris moved his hand."

"It wouldn't be unusual for him to move. Your friend is in a deep sleep, but he is by no means dead. The body is alive, it's only his mind that's resting. And a living body tends to move."

"Are you okay?" the younger nurse asked. "Can I bring you some water?"

"No, thank you."

"Call me if there's anything you need," she said and winked. The older nurse sighed and stormed out of the room.

"Thank you."

The younger nurse joined her.

I looked at Boris. "You bastard. You are up to mischief even when you're in a coma."

I went over to the window and looked at the people in front of the hospital, walking in and out of the building like an army of ants. Patients, doctors, nurses, technicians, maintenance workers, visitors. For a moment I even noticed a specific pattern in their movements. Each one of them was moving in a predetermined direction, towards a clearly defined goal. In and out. Out and in. From the ones who reached the street, some turned left, some turned right, while others crossed the road. They were then divided into those who turned right and went towards the bus stop, those who turned left and went to their parked cars, and those who continued straight on and entered the tobacconist's. In the other direction, the situation was not as diverse. They were all marching towards a single goal. Everybody was walking - except for her. She stood out in her red jacket, in the middle of the clearing, looking around. The masses did not pull her in and she did not join the rest in their movements. She was a flaw in the system and she was aware of it. She calmly observed her co-inhabitants on this crazy planet and smiled. She was alone with her thoughts. Alone amongst people.

CHAPTER NINE

Horvat called me in the evening to ask about my wellbeing. He told me they had tracked down the murder weapon, but he did not want to give up any details. He suggested that I should take few days off from work. I thanked him for his concern, but I explained that taking some time off would only make it all worse. He replied by saying that he needed me back on top of things and hinted that I had no say in the matter. I said goodbye and put the cell phone on the kitchen counter. I took a can of beer from the fridge. What a day I thought to myself as I opened the beer and took two long gulps. Sara was having dinner with her girlfriends. I was not hungry even though I only had a chocolate croissant for breakfast. I turned my computer on. I had not logged onto Facebook for ages and looked a bit surprised when I saw a multitude of green messenger lights. It was Friday night and the number of people wanting to chat reflected this. It did not take long before a chat window appeared in the lower corner. Andrea, a fellow student from Uni, wanted to talk. We had a two-week fling during which we had never made it to bed. That was probably because she had had a boyfriend and did not want to cheat on him. Or maybe it was because she started talking about marriage on our second date. And she got it. Of course, she did not marry me, nor the guy she was with at the time, for reasons that elude me. Life is like a night swim. Despite your fear of the unknown and the darkness below, you just jump into the pitch black water and start swimming. Although one has to admit that most of the time when you go for a dip like that, you are horny as hell and not sober at all.

"Hi, Rok. How are you? I haven't seen you on Facebook for ages, so when I saw your name pop up I just had to click on it. I hope I'm not interrupting anything."

"Hi. I've been better. What about you?"

"Oh no. I'm okay, thanks for asking. Are you and Sara still together?"

Straight to the point. Things have certainly changed since Uni.

"Yup. What about you and … What's his name?"

I do not know who she married in the end and to tell you the truth I did not even care.

"Marjan. We're getting divorced. It didn't work out."

This is what happens when you are in a hurry to get married at twenty-five.

"Fuck. Sorry to hear that."

I really could not care less.

"Thank you, but it's better this way. We weren't meant to be together."

Very insightful of her. Especially, because it only took them six years and two children to figure out that they were not a match.

"I never stopped thinking about you."

"Really?"

"Yeah. It still bums me out that it never worked out between us."

Babe, you were hanging out with me for two weeks just to make your boyfriend jealous. Did not work out?! I think it worked out exactly as you planned.

"To be completely honest, it worked out flawlessly for me. I'm delighted to be with Sara."

She started typing and then stopped. And again and again and a few more times. And then the green light next to her name suddenly disappeared. Interesting. I lit a cigarette and started googling what the machine for measuring heart rates is called. I was still browsing when I heard another ping. I was no longer in the mood to talk to Andrea, but I looked anyway and noticed that a second chat window had popped up. It was Tina.

"Hi, Rok. Are you okay?"

"Hi, Tina. Relatively okay. I visited Boris today."

"I've heard the chances that he will wake up are pretty slim."

"He moved his hand. But they said it was a muscle spasm or something."

"I prayed for him yesterday."

"I didn't know you were religious."

"I'm not… But it can't do any harm I suppose."

The green light reappeared in the other window. Andrea came back from her virtual timeout.

"Sorry. I had to go for a smoke."

"No worries. Are you okay?"

"Horvat told me you'll take a few days off. Shall we meet for a coffee, or something stronger?"

"I'm not okay. I'm getting a divorce."

"Love to. Shall we meet in Prulček in half an hour?"

"Andrea, do you think you rushed into marriage?"

"I was planning to do some yoga, but I'm happy to ditch that plan and grab a beer with you instead."

"I always wanted to marry you."

My god. I have to nip this in the bud.

"Hehe. OK."

"Listen to me, we were never a couple. We didn't even have a fling. We made out a couple of times, and that was all."

"I'm going to hit the shower, see you soon."

"I'm lonely."

"There's nothing I can do to help you."

"I'm horny."

Ten years ago you did not want to show me your

boobs when you had a chance to.

"Can't help you with that either."

The green light disappeared again. Facebook is like walking through a labyrinth with a magic wand in your pocket. When you get lost, you just wave your digital magic stick, and you will be back in reality in no time. As if nothing ever happened. In this parallel universe, you can chat with your ex-lovers and talk to them about the lost opportunities and life's tragedies. The bolder take a step further and upload an intimate photograph onto the ever-hungry servers. Then they return to their home base and cook dinner for their partners and children. Only to head to work the very next day, pretending that nothing unusual is going on. And in this tangible reality of ours, that's actually true.

* * *

Tina was the first one to arrive to Prulček. Of course she sat outside, as any smoker would. When she saw me, she stood up and waved. She was wearing a pair of torn jeans and a white knitted pullover. She looked exceptionally hot. We hugged and sat down.

"You look well," I said.

"Thank you. So do you. But you know that. How are you?"

"I'm fine. Surprisingly fine."

I wasn't lying, I felt exceptionally strong.

"What can I get you?" asked the waiter who suddenly appeared next to the table. I looked at Tina and indicated with my eyes that she should order first.

"Bernard. Lager."

The waiter looked at me.

"A Porter and a Jameson on the rocks."

"I'll have a Jameson too," added Tina.

The waiter nodded and stormed towards the bar.

"I couldn't believe it when I saw you on Facebook. You are never online."

"True. And now I know why. I was online for five minutes, and a friend from Uni already started chatting me up."

"Which one?"

"Andrea. I don't think you know her."

"Andrea Plevnik?"

"Yes. How…"

"We know each other from aerobics classes. She once mentioned the two of you were an item at Uni and…"

"An item? We were more like fuck buddies who never fucked. You could say that we were friends with benefits and that we never enjoyed those benefits." I had to smile.

"Wait a minute. You were together at University, and you never slept together? Now that is an achievement."

The waiter brought the drinks and a bowl of peanuts.

"I'm telling you, we've never been an item. We made out at one of those student parties after she'd been pestering me all evening. Afterward, we went out a couple of times, and I went to her place once …"

"Wait a second. You were at her place? Alone? And you didn't fuck her? Did she have her period or were you too drunk to get it up?"

Tina has always been very direct.

"I don't remember what the reason was. What I do know is that she used me to make her boyfriend jealous and that it was all a bit weird."

"Whoa. She had a boyfriend? So you were the lover, and you didn't get to take a swing at her? Well, that's the first time I've heard a story like that and I've heard a lot of stories."

"Well, that's the way the cookie crumbled. And yes, it's a fact that I dated a woman who had a boyfriend and that we didn't have sex. And that's the bottom line."

"It sounds pretty fucked up to me. I'll drink to that. Cheers!"

She raised the glass towards me. We clinked our glasses together, and we each took a sip.

"You want to hear about another fucked up situation? But you have got to keep this to yourself. You have to promise not to tell anyone."

She sat still for approximately three seconds and then she pulled her fingers across her lips as if she was zipping them shut.

"Not a word. I promise."

I told her about the diary that had appeared on my computer. I explained everything down to the very last detail. She listened with her mouth wide open, and I could see in her eyes that she believed me. Well, the story was so inconceivable that it would have been impossible to make it up on the spot. When I finished my story, I grabbed hold of my glass and poured its content down the hatch. Ah, burning ecstasy with instantaneous results.

"What do you think the guys of the forensic department will find?"

"I have no idea. But whatever they might find will be better than what I have to go on now. At the moment I'm just stumbling through the dark."

"So you genuinely believe that you are writing the diary?"

"I strongly suspect that this is the case, yes."

"It sounds insane."

She grabbed a couple of peanuts and carried them to her mouth one by one.

"I've heard some crazy stuff in my life, but never anything as surreal as this."

"I know."

"I know someone who might be able to help you."

"Just don't tell me that I should visit a gypsy woman who sees things in a crystal ball."

She laughed.

"Don't be ridiculous. My friend Klemen is a hypnotist.

39

He's had quite a few weird cases so far. You've got nothing to lose by popping round his place. I think I have his telephone number…"

Hypnosis, I thought. I immediately saw the scenes from television, in which hypnotized people performed absurd tasks, while the audience in the studio was rolling with laughter. I always believed that such scenes were scripted like American wrestling which I loved watching when I was a child. I also heard that some people changed after they were hypnotized and that one person had ended up in a psychiatric hospital once. I did not personally know anyone who had been hypnotized, but the very idea of hypnosis made me anxious. Some people do not believe hypnosis is possible, but I consider it an exceptionally powerful tool that can help us gain insight into the human subconscious. I am not scared of it. I have a certain respect for it. Both for hypnosis and the people who practice it.

"Thanks, but I think I'll wait for the forensic results. There is still the possibility that someone is just screwing with me."

"Of course, I understand. Well, if you decide that you want to see him, I have his telephone number."

"Thanks. Do you want another?" I pointed at the almost empty glass.

"Oh yes."

* * *

Four beers, three whiskeys, and one espresso later I sat in the living room, staring at the television that was turned off. I was not too drunk because I had constantly been drinking water with my alcohol. Tina was good company, as usual. During our conversation, we discussed her recent flings, current films, and books that we should read. We toasted Quentin Tarantino's birthday. We ordered a pizza. During the last round, we discussed the meaning of life, the endless universe and the cosmic mistake that is known as mankind. I took the opportunity and revealed to her my theory that the Moon is not the Earth's natural satellite, but some sort of a projection. If the Moon is truly spinning around its axis, how come we always see the same side? How is this possible? According to the general consensus, the Moon's path runs in sync with the spinning of the Earth, which is why we always see the same side. But let us dig a bit deeper. When looking into the sky, the Moon appears to be exactly as big as the sun. This is clearly seen whenever there is a total eclipse of the sun. The Moon is also precisely the right distance from the Earth for the Earth's shadow to totally cover the Moon during a lunar eclipse. I think there are too many coincidences for this to not be suspicious. Of course, I also mentioned that the Apollo 11 Moon landing, in 1969, was faked and recorded in a studio with help from Stanley Kubrick. I also told her about my assumption that I believe it is impossible for rockets to leave the Earth's orbit and that space travel is a scam. Tina listened to me carefully, nodded a few times, and then said: "You are really something." No, I am not. It just amazes me how much crap the media, the internet, and so-called scientists keep serving us on a daily basis. It is unbelievable that they can still bypass our intellect, logic and instincts. They are screwing with our minds all the time, and we even thank them for the revelations that they have given us. Science ceased to be the driving force behind mankind. It is an iron clog that prevents us from moving forward.

CHAPTER TEN

I opened my eyes on Saturday morning. I had fallen asleep on the sofa. The aroma of French toast was wafting in from the kitchen, and I could hear Adele singing.

"Morning!" I yelled into the unknown.

"Good morning!" came Sara's response a few seconds later.

She stepped into the living room dressed in a grey tracksuit, a short black T-shirt, and a white apron.

"I didn't want to wake you up."

"You didn't."

"Did you sleep well?"

"Okay. But I had some weird dreams. Boris and I were sitting on a bench next to the Ljubljanica River, drinking beer on a gorgeous sunny day. Everything was great. We were talking about this and that, and having a few laughs. All of a sudden I asked him: "Aren't you dead?" and he replied: "Yes, this is it.""

"That's insane. I just remembered I forgot to ask you yesterday. Where's your laptop? Don't tell me it was stolen again."

"No, no. I took it to forensics. They'll give me a call later on today and tell me what they've come up with."

"Great. I hope they'll get to the bottom of it."

"Me too."

A part of me hoped that it was not a prank. I wanted it to be real. I hoped somebody, most likely me, was sending these messages from the future. Do they not relate to the childhood dreams we all had? Did we not dream that we could travel in time? We all certainly wanted to know what the future had in store for us. The people betting on sports would kill to have access to that kind of information. Well, at least the honest ones, who were not fixing the results. I have occasionally placed a few bets in my lifetime. The last time was in a casino three years ago. I put a five euro chip on number thirteen at the roulette, won, stopped betting, and subsequently ended at the height of my gambling career, like a real champion. It was not about the money, it was about the principle of the matter. Just like my bowling career. After twelve years I, at the peak of my strength and form, decided to end my commitment to the sport. I had already competed at the youth world championships, and I had almost made it to the national team. If I had put in a bit more effort, I could have become a world-class bowler, but I opted to go into a different direction, and I bade farewell to the sport while I was on top. A strike. My last throw was a strike. A perfect farewell. I think I made the right decision. I always look back on bowling fondly, and it never bores me. I still enjoy reading articles about the successes of my former colleagues that I have bowled tens of thousands of balls with and knocked down countless pins. We always knew how to celebrate our victories in the wildest ways.

"The French toast is delicious," I said, stuffing the second slice into my mouth. Sara was an excellent cook, who preferred simple food. Occasionally she surrendered to the temptation of experimental culinary delicacies in exquisite restaurants. But neither of us could understand the sudden appearance of beds of arugula, ever smaller portions, the molecular kitchen and specialties like rooster crown. Personally, I swear by a good steak and roasted potatoes, pizza or pasta. Considering the sort of food that I ate, I was damn lucky my diet was not reflected in a layer of fatty cells covering my entire body. I guess my metabolism must be extremely efficient.

"Thank you darling. Do you want another one?"

"Sure thing. I'm starving. Is there any more coffee?"

"I can always make some."

"You don't need to make it just for me."

"Don't be ridiculous. Of course I'll make it just for you."

"You really are the best."

I sprinkled some sugar on a golden slice of French toast. Food fit for gods I thought. I sat on the terrace and lit a cigarette while holding a second cup of coffee in my hand. Sara was washing the dishes. For the second day in a row, I could see a red Renault Clio parked on the sidewalk across the street. You can not even rely on tow trucks these days. I remembered the day my car was towed for the first time. It was autumn, 2006 or 2007. At the time, I had a fourth generation VW Golf. I only had it for about a week, when I had arranged to meet an old friend, whom I had not seen in years, for coffee. I parked in a parking space reserved for taxis in front of Le Petit Café and walked towards Premier, which was where we had arranged to meet. An hour or two later, I was standing in front of an empty parking space wondering what had happened to my box on wheels. First, I thought it had been stolen. When your car is towed, they do not leave a note letting you know what happened. Instead, they leave you wondering. Luckily, they already had a website at the time, and they used it to publish the license plate numbers of the vehicles that they towed to their depot on the outskirts of town. I sat in the garden of Le Petit Café, ordered another coffee and looked at their page. At the very end of the list, I found my license plate, LJ T8-13J. It seemed that I would have to raid a cash machine as quickly as possible and head for the depot. I decided to walk there to clear my head. Fuck. I have no idea how long it took me to get there, but the Road of the Two Emperors felt like the longest road in Ljubljana.

Sara joined me on the terrace. I asked her about dinner and mentioned that I had met Tina for a drink.

"I told her about the diary."

"And?"

"Nothing. I think that she believed me."

"Believed what?"

"That it's me writing it."

"Oh my god Rok, don't tell me you actually believe that."

"What should I believe? That gnomes crawl around my computer and predict what will happen to me the next day, while I'm sleeping?"

"Don't be stupid."

"I'm not stupid. It's all clear. My laptop includes a Word document that I didn't create, and I'm most definitely not writing it, nor are you, but it's updated every day and describes what will actually happen the next day. These are the facts. These are the undeniable facts."

"Look, we've discussed this before. Your computer might have been hacked. Wait for what Forensics has to say. When are they supposed to get back to you?"

"This afternoon."

"Wait until then. Don't make your conclusions before they got back to you. I'm sure that they'll find out who's behind it."

Cause and effect. Diametrically opposing notions and yet one does not exist without the other. It is one of the Universal constants. Action and reaction. Cause and effect."

"Do you want to come to the market with me?"

Sara's voice immediately broke my line of thought.

I looked at her.

"Eh?"

"I'm going to the market. Do you want to join me?"

I'm not the greatest fan of the crowds at the market, but I could go for a walk.

"I'm coming. But I need to brush my teeth first."

"No need to hurry. I'll check the fridge to see what we need."

CHAPTER ELEVEN

At two fifteen, while Sara was preparing lunch for the two of us, I received a phone call from Peter. Anxiously I pressed the green button on my phone's screen.

"Peter! What do you have?"

"Hi, Rok. I have the results of the tests that we carried out on your laptop."

"And?"

"Can you come over?"

"Have you found anything?"

"It would be best if you came over. Something strange is happening, and I'm not comfortable discussing it over the phone."

"I'll be there in twenty minutes."

"Okay. I'll wait for you in my office."

"What's happening?" Sara asked from the kitchen.

"It seems as if the guys from Forensics found something. I have to come over."

"Aren't you going to have something to eat before you go?"

"I've suddenly lost my appetite."

"I understand. Go. You'll eat when you come back."

I kissed her and put on my jeans and my gray jacket. I grabbed the car keys from the stand in the hall and looked over at Sara again. She was smiling.

"Everything will be fine," she said. "I told you that they'll get to the bottom of it."

"I can't remember the last time when I was this nervous."

"Go!"

I opened the front door and stood still on the doorstep for a moment or two. Took a deep breath and looked towards the sky. I could hear a song by Niet playing in my head.

* * *

"Take a seat, Rok" said Peter as soon as I entered his office.

His face looked stern, it was not often that anyone saw him as grim as this.

"What's happening?" I asked.

"We conducted a complete forensic investigation of your laptop and thoroughly analyzed the hardware as well as the software. My best experts worked on your case."

"And what have they found?"

"Apart from the hidden porn?" he smiled.

"Stop beating around the bush, Peter. Tell me what you've found."

"Okay. I just wanted to lighten up the situation."

"That's okay."

"First the physical analysis. We have found fingerprints belonging to two people on your laptop."

He paused for a while.

"Mine and Sara's?"

"That's right."

"Fuck."

"Were you expecting that we'd find more?"

"I'm not sure."

"Okay, let's continue. We checked the hardware. We didn't find any irregularities. Everything is exactly as it's supposed to be."

"So basically my computer has not been physically altered. That must mean it has been hacked."

"Do you want a glass of whiskey?"

"No thanks. But I'd like to find out what the hell is going on."

"Of course. Sorry. Let's move on. We also analyzed the software and the network connections. We checked every path that could've been used to break into your computer. As I've said, my best experts were on the case. There is nobody better …"

"Are you trying to tell me they haven't found anything?"

"I think I need some whiskey. Are you sure you don't want some?"

I shook my head. He walked to the wooden cabinet and took a bottle of Chivas from it. A healthy amount cascaded from the bottle into the glass that he was holding. He immediately gulped down its contents in a single go, as if he was drinking iced tea.

"Where did we leave off? Ah, yes, the analysis. Nobody broke into your computer. Everything seems to be normal. As I've said, the best experts were working on it. They used the best, most up-to-date software and came up with nothing."

He poured another glass of whiskey for himself, this time the dose was not as generous.

"Until this morning."

"What?!"

He drank from his glass.

"A new entry appeared in the file this morning."

"Have you read it?"

"Yes."

"What does it say?"

"Wait a sec."

Peter opened the door.

"Domen. Domen!"

An overweight technician with a goatee and a buzz cut, wearing a white lab coat, looked up from his computer screen.

"Could you please bring sample R1-244."

"Is that the one that writes by itself?"

"Yes. Can you just bring it please."

Domen brought the laptop wrapped in plastic foil. Peter unwrapped it, placed it in front of me and turned it on. When the familiar desktop appeared, I clicked on the icon that opened the mysterious diary. The Word document opened. I scrolled to the end of it and noticed a new entry. I started reading.

March 28, 2015

I woke up on the couch, without a hangover. I told Tina about the diary yesterday, and she said it was a good idea. She said that keeping a journal has helped her and that it eventually transformed into some sort of self-therapy. I decided to continue writing, at least for as long as I have something to say. I dreamt about Boris last night. We were sitting on a bench next to the river, talking. At one point I asked him: "Aren't you dead?" and he replied: "Yes, this is it." What does that mean? Is he dead or am I dead? Are we all dead and merely deceived by the illusion that we are alive? Are dreams an extension of physical reality, or is our external reality a dream? Who knows? I think somebody has hacked my laptop. If you're reading this, you should know that I'll track you down.

"I think I'll have some of that whiskey now."

"At the time this entry was added, nobody was accessing your laptop. Nobody had access from here, nor from the outside."

"A text can't write itself."

I swallowed the whiskey.

"It didn't write itself."

"What do you mean?"

"The text was written on your computer."

"What are you trying to say?"

"It's simple. Somebody typed it on your laptop's keyboard."

"Peter, don't screw around with me."

"I am not messing with you. The keyboard was cleaned

yesterday evening. And in the morning, when we discovered the new entry ..."

"What?"

"Well, when we discovered the new entry, we checked for fingerprints again."

"And?"

"We found a new set of fingerprints on the keyboard."

"Whose?"

"Yours."

Darkness fell upon me. My hope for clarity faded instantly.

"That's impossible. I was at home. I mean at the market. Anyway, I wasn't here."

"I know."

"So what's your explanation?"

"I have no explanation. This is the craziest thing I've ever seen in my life. And that's not all ..."

"There's more? Please, tell me."

"Technically the text has not been written yet."

"What do you mean? I just read it."

"Each file has its own timestamp. A timestamp tells us when a file has been updated. Even if you, for instance, change the time on your computer, the timestamp always shows the exact time when the file was created or updated. This file was updated today."

"I thought we already knew that. You told me the update appeared this morning."

"No, today at six in the afternoon. Four minutes past six in the afternoon to be precise."

"Fuck. How is this possible?"

"It's not. It is virtually impossible to manipulate a timestamp."

"That means that I wrote this entry three hours from now?"

"Sort of - yes."

"But I don't even keep a diary."

"I think I'll start writing one today. Do you want

another whiskey?"

* * *

"How is that possible? Are you sure somebody isn't toying with you?"

Sara has an open mind, but most of the time her cautious skepticism was not too far away.

"Peter says it's impossible to change a file's timestamp. He couldn't explain how my fingerprints appeared on a clean keyboard, on a computer that was securely locked away and not touched by anyone either."

"There must be a logical explanation for it all."

"I think logic fails us in this case. We are beyond all reason, and it's time for us to start using our imagination."

I looked at the computer and then at the sizable clock hanging on the living room wall. Two minutes to six. The entry from the future was merely six minutes away. I imagined I was sitting at the desk in the study, thinking about what to write. I had never kept a diary, which meant that my alter ego differed in this aspect. And yet he lived in the same world, worked in the same profession and was surrounded by the same people. His days were exactly the same as mine. The only difference was that he was recording them in this perplexing diary. Well, at least he has been doing this over the last few days. Was he aware that I was reading his records? Is he keeping the diary just so that I can read it? Is he trying to warn me about something?

Suddenly, a crazy idea came to me. I leaped towards the laptop and opened it. I opened the file with the diary and read the last sentence.

If you're reading this, you should know I'll track you down.

My hands trembled as I started typing.

I'm here. I'm reading. What's the point of all this?

I saved the file.

"Babe, what are you up to?"

"I'm communicating."

"With whom?"

"Well, with myself to be honest. I just thought that this computer communication might go both ways. Maybe I can talk to him, myself, well you know what I mean."

"So you're saying you're trying to write to your future self? Please don't tell anyone." Sara sneered at me.

"Go ahead and make a fool of me, but I believe this might work."

"How would it work exactly?"

"I'm not sure. When he decides to write something new, he'll open the document with my text in it."

"Hmm, interesting. I still think it's a crazy idea."

"Crazier than reading a diary written by me in the future?"

"You're right. Curiously enough, your theory actually makes sense."

CHAPTER TWELVE

As soon as I opened my eyes, I stumbled towards the computer. When I saw the new entry at the end of the document my heart started pounding.

March 29, 2015
Sunday started off like any old Sunday. Sara and I had sex in the shower. I adore her. Not only her body and her magnificent mind but everything she represents. The best humanity has to offer is embodied by her. Hardly a day goes by without me thanking the universe for bringing us together. Life is good.

This is where the entry stopped. It seemed he had not read my response. I looked at the previous page.

If you're reading this, you should know I'll track you down.

And that was it. My response wasn't there. Did he delete it after seeing it? Perhaps my assumptions were wrong. Maybe the communication does not work both ways. Whatever it might be, it was obvious that his universe was not the same as mine. My Sunday had not started with sex.

"Rok, are you going to join me in the shower?"

Welcome to the Twilight Zone, I said to myself as I slowly made my way to the bathroom.

* * *

Life takes place on so many different levels, it is impossible to imagine them all. There are seven billion people on this spherical rock. That is seven billion different perspectives, seven billion truths, seven billion autonomous thoughts. Imagine that you are walking down the street, watching people as they walk towards you. You see them from your perspective. There is a mother with a baby, a guy with a mustache who is watching them on their left. Two female students are laughing happily as they pass all three of them, walking in your direction. You might stop to wonder what made them so cheerful. Did they just receive their exam results and pass them? Or did one of their idols comment on one of their photographs on Instagram? Do they like me? What are they talking about? A student party? Are they discussing what they will have for lunch? All of these thoughts run through your head, while the mom's thoughts are focused on entirely different things. She might be wondering whether her child's diaper is full again, although she changed it before leaving home about half an hour ago. Or she might be wondering whether it is worth staying with her husband who has started behaving differently ever since the baby was born. The man with the mustache is most likely fantasizing about having sex with her, or he might be reminiscing how delightful it was when he became a father for the first time. All of this is being observed simultaneously by the lady who is watering her flowers, on the balcony across the street, and her husband who is standing on the opposite side of it, smoking a cigarette. They have an almost identical view of the events below them, and yet they both see them in their own way. Seven people, seven different outlooks on the same moment in time. Now multiply this by a billion. It is a terrifying number of viewpoints, truths, and thoughts, is it not? And then there are animals, each one with its own view of the world and life. There are supposedly twenty quintillion animals on this planet. That is twenty billion billion lives. And each one of them has a distinctive conception of the biosphere that they inhabit. It is possible that the vast majority of them do not contemplate their existence, but this does not change the fact that they perceive their surroundings and respond to them in accordance with their capabilities. And then there are plants, which one might find hard to call beings but are undoubtedly alive, bacteria and viruses. Finally there is a world that we do not consider to be living. Such an abundance of life. So, remember what a weak link in the chain you are, the next time a microscopic virus forces you to stay in bed.

* * *

We had run out of coffee, so I suggested to Sara that we would take a walk to the town center and stop in Chokl for a cup as they have fantastic, home roasted coffee there. We walked along the river, past Trta and Rupel's villa, crossed the road at St. Jacob's Bridge and entered the old town center.

"This is new."

Sara pointed to the left, towards a gallery which had obviously opened very recently.

"What was here before?"

"I think it was some sort of fast food place or something," she guessed.

"I think it was an empty shop. If my memory serves me right, this place used to be all boarded up."

"You could be right. It's nice to see it was given a new lease of life."

We continued walking through the old town and strolled around the fountain on Gornji Square. As we continued our way down the road, we passed two restaurants, that are on opposite sides of the street, named Romeo and Juliet. Shortly after, we walked by Ljubljana's city hall, which has a replica of Robba's Fountain in front of it and continued our way past the cathedral. Finally, we wandered past the marketplace and went right past Vodnikov Hram until we arrived at Chokl.

"Oh, look! It's Rok and Sara," Tine, the cafe owner greeted us.

"Hi, Tine."

"It seems rather empty today," Sara said observingly.

"It's a beautiful day, so most people went to the seaside. What can I get you?"

"What's your special blend today?" I asked.

"A Ugandan and Mexican blend."

"Is it any good?"

"Have you ever drunk a bad cup of coffee at my place?"

"Never. I'll have a coffee with milk."

"And I'll have that air-press or whatever it's called," Sara surprised me.

Tine nodded and went back inside.

"Whoa, that'll be your second coffee of the day. Living on the edge, eh?" I said, trying to be clever.

"You don't go to a butcher's shop to buy screws, do you?"

Boom, touché.

"True. Do you have a lighter?"

I lit up a cigarette.

"Can I have one? I forgot mine at home."

I pushed the box towards her.

"You can have two if you want."

After a few moments of pleasant silence, I blurted out, "Yesterday I tried the thing I mentioned I might try."

"Eh?"

"I wrote in the diary. But it obviously didn't work. There was a new entry in the morning, but my text had been deleted."

"What did it say?"

"What did I write?"

"Yes."

"I told him that I'm reading his entries. I asked him what's the point."

"And what did he write?"

"That we had sex in the shower."

Another few seconds of silence.

"I've been thinking about it. It sounds unbelievable, but it's the only possible explanation," Sara said.

"What is?"

"That you are writing the diary in the future or in a parallel universe."

"Crazy, isn't it?"

"Totally off the charts crazy. But just because something is unbelievable, that doesn't mean it's impossible."

"Nothing's impossible," I replied.

"Well, I wouldn't go that far."

"But why me?"

"Someone has to be the first. Do you think you're less important than other people?"

"No. I don't know. Importance is a relative concept."

"If we're on the topic of relativity, everything's relative."

"That's true. Are you aware of what we have on my laptop?"

"A portal that transcends the boundaries of time and space?"

"Or a crystal ball. We are the first people in history who can actually see what's going to happen in the future."

"You don't know that. But, If you want to predict the future, you should have ordered Turkish coffee." Sara uttered.

"Oh c'mon. Don't tell me you believe in fortune telling?"

"I thought nothing was impossible."

"Telling your future from coffee grounds seems damn

close to impossible."

"You can't think something is stupid just because you don't understand it. Well, it doesn't matter, for all I know we can even predict the future with the sugar if we wanted to," Sara replied sarcastically, and both of us laughed.

Tine suddenly appeared with two cups of coffee, and put an end to our discussion.

* * *

In the evening, while Sara was ironing, I rechecked the diary. The time was right – it was ten minutes past seven, which was about the time new records usually appeared. But there was nothing. I reread the entire text from the very beginning right to the end. Everything that was jotted down had actually taken place. I was trying to figure out whether there was a way for me to communicate with my future self. Should I leave him a post-it on the fridge? Write something on the board in the hallway? Write a letter? I shook my head. What was I thinking? How could I possibly send a letter to my future double? The postman would just bring it to me the next day. The diary was the only medium that I could use to communicate with him, but it apparently only works in one direction. But that is illogical. My future is mine and mine alone. It has not occurred yet. My future is also the past of the future me. If I do something in my present moment, it will not show up on his radar. And vice versa. And yet, I was looking at a document that challenged my assumptions. A day-by-day account that surpassed temporal and spatial restrictions. Does he know I am reading his diary? I guess not, otherwise he would be writing it differently. Could the journal, if I started writing it, be read by my past self? What makes my laptop so unique? How come this is possible? Why me? Do you think you're less important than other people? I believe that there are people who are more intelligent and better qualified for this. I silenced my inner voice with a glass of red wine.

"Do you want some wine?" I shouted towards the bedroom.

"Of course I do. I'll be right there."

I took another glass from the cupboard, wiped it off with a cloth and poured the intoxicating red liquid into it. Then I just stared at the glass with a vacant mind. This was one of my most important talents. I knew how to switch off my insatiably curious brain. Many men probably know how to do this, but I always led myself on to believe that I was the only one.

"Hey, have you read the new entry?!"

"What? What new entry? There's none."

"Look."

Two seconds later I was staring at the computer screen, hastily reading the words that had just appeared.

March 30, 2015

Life happens as you walk down the street and the phone rings. Literally. Sara is pregnant. It didn't come as an absolute surprise seeing as we never use condoms, but we never planned on having a child.

I looked at Sara.

"I'm a week late."

I had no idea how to respond and continued reading.

I was overflowing with emotions that were previously unknown to me. In a brief moment, I tried to call Boris, but I returned to the real world a second later and hung up before the first ring.

"Have you taken a pregnancy test?"

"Not yet. I thought it was because of all the stress at work."

"Should I rush out to the drugstore?"

"Leave it. I'll get it tomorrow on my way to work."

"This is a pretty strange way to find out."

"Let's wait for the test results. Have you read the diary to the end?"

I noticed there was another sentence at the end.

Tu fui, ego eris.

"I don't understand it. Is it Latin?"

"Yes."

"Wait, I'll google it."

"You don't have to. I know what it means."

"Well c'mon, tell me."

"What you are, I was. What I am, you will be."

I stood up, stumbled across the living room and fell onto the sofa.

"Are you alright?"

Sara sat down next to me and rested her head on my shoulder.

"He knows."

"Who knows?"

"Him. Me. He knows I'm reading what he writes. I mean I'm reading what I write. Well, you know what I'm trying to say."

"What are you going to do?"

"What can I do? I tried writing in his diary, but he obviously couldn't read what I wrote."

"And what would you say to him if you could establish contact with him?"

"I have no idea."

"There you go. Relax and enjoy the current reality of knowing what will happen to you tomorrow. People would kill for this."

"You're right."

"I'm always right. You should know that by now. Shall we go to bed? I want to make it to the office early, and I still have to pass a drugstore on the way tomorrow morning."

At that moment I returned to the present.

"Err, congratulations."

"You should congratulate yourself, silly. You're the one who pulled out a bit too late."

CHAPTER THIRTEEN

I opened my eyes and reminisced about the strange dream that had come to me last night. I was sitting in the living room, talking to myself. Not with myself as myself, but with my counterpart from the future. I can not remember what we were talking about, but I remember what he said to me just before I woke up.

"We come in infinite numbers and there used to be even more of us."

I parked in front of Ljubljana's Police headquarters. There was nobody outside. I lit a cigarette. *We come in infinite numbers.* I knew he was talking about me. About us. An infinite number of Rok Kopitars living in various versions of the present. *And there used to be even more of us.* That sounds logical. Some died. I tried to recollect how many times I might have stared death in the face. In some realities, I had probably died. I have often thought about parallel universes, and this diary was irrefutable proof that they exist. And more. It is proof that contact can be established between parallel universes or, more precisely, between parallel lives. Dreams. Dreams could be our primary portal through which we enter our parallel lives. Sometimes we dream about a homelike, comfortable environment and people we are familiar with from our personal lives, but at other times our dreams take place in an unknown environment with people we do not know. Is it possible that they offer us a glimpse of our parallel lives? Perhaps some of those lives are close, even similar to our actual experience while others are more remote. Thus, essentially different. I bet that this is plausible, but I could be wrong. But even if the potential for something is infinitesimal, it is an indisputable fact that there are only two possibilities. Something either is, or it is not. On that note, I put out my cigarette and entered the building.

* * *

"They say he can breathe on his own and that there's a good chance he'll wake up within the next few days," said Horvat.

"That's great news!"

"I have more good news. We know who was behind it."

"Who?"

"Take it easy. You know I can't tell you. I would hate to see you do something stupid."

"Simon, you know me. You know I wouldn't do anything without orders."

"I know how close you are to Boris. I know you would do anything to get back at the perpetrator in revenge for the murder of Milena. Even I would if I were in your shoes. I can't let you be a part of this. You understand, don't you?"

"I do. Just promise me we'll get the bastard."

"We'll nail him. In the meantime, I want you back on the Walter case, or Operation Orion Pax as it'll be known from now on. I've already told Interpol's Albert Nolan that you're on the team."

Nolan. It has apparently been decided that this case is going to be handled meticulously. Albert Nolan was the great white shark of detectives. Since his arrival at the drug task force, the number of cases solved had doubled. The only blemish on his impeccable career was the mysterious disappearance of Madeleine McCann in 2007. Nolan took this failure personally and had asked to be transferred in

2010.

"I assume Walter isn't Nolan's main target," I said.

"You know the stakes have reached new highs when the big boys are invited along to play."

"Rock 'n' roll."

My phone rang as I was walking towards the Union restaurant on Nazorjeva Street where I had arranged to meet a colleague.

"Hi, sweetie. I took the pregnancy test. Well, I took two, just to be on the safe side."

"And?"

"Both of them were positive."

This came as no surprise, but I felt a sudden surge of happiness. It is only once in a lifetime that you become a father for the first time.

"That's fantastic news! I'll take you out for dinner, and we'll celebrate tonight."

"I'm already looking forward to it."

I was staring at the phone, trying to resist my overwhelming desire to call my wingman. I knew that I wanted to call Boris first and tell him about the exciting news, but I also knew that he was unable to answer his phone. I placed the cell phone back into my pocket and entered the restaurant. My life, like so many times before, has taken a step into the unknown. However, this time, I will walk this path with a map. A map of my life. That would be an excellent title for a movie.

* * *

"C'mon, not Bruno!" I was appalled.

"Why not? Bruno is a wonderful name," Sara persisted.

"Bruno Kopitar? It just doesn't work."

"What about Oliver?"

"Don't tell me you want his initials to be OK."

"Now you are just being ridiculous."

"What about Ivan?"

"Ivan sounds good…for a seventy-year-old man."

"Zeus?"

"Don't be stupid."

"What if it's a girl?" I tried to deflect the discussion as it was not going anywhere.

"Zoe."

"Ella?"

"Tara."

"Lea?"

"Nea."

Joe Peña's was packed. I think we were one of the few guests not paying with student food coupons. I was still holding a grudge against the restaurant for recently serving me awful guacamole. I was not as bothered about the sauce as I was by the annoying attitude of the waiter who tried to convince me that it was precisely the way it was supposed to be. He claimed that he had tried it, the cook had tried it, even the cleaning lady had tried it, and it was definitely the way it was supposed to be. Sara was the one who they had to thank for this customer returning to this establishment. Come to think of it, if I had not pulled out too late, I probably would have never set foot in this restaurant again. Fortunately, the guacamole did not taste like the inside of a dirty toilet bowl this time.

"I think we have plenty of time to decide on a name. We should wait until we know whether it's a boy or a girl."

"Always the voice of reason," said Sara. "Do you want some dessert?"

"I think I'm stuffed."

"OK, you'll get dessert at home."

"Check please!" I yelled at the waitress.

* * *

March 31, 2015
Boris woke up.

I saw that the text continued, but I only read the first sentence. A million thoughts rushed through my head. Boris is awake. Well, actually, Boris will be awake soon. What will he say when he sees me? Will he be the same old Boris? Does he know who shot him? When he comes to, will he think of Milena first? Does he know Milena is dead? There were millions of questions and only one solution. I went to the kitchen and poured myself a double dose of Jameson, took a big swig of it, grabbed my laptop and went to the terrace. I lit a cigarette and continued reading.

I was swarmed with feelings that were impossible to describe when I heard Horvat say those three words over the phone. I will speak to my friend in a few hours' time, a friend I believed to be gone forever. He will probably not be the same. It is said that a close encounter with death will mark you forever. As I don't have this experience, I don't know what it's really like. But I can imagine it. At some point in time, we all become aware of our own mortality. Someone once told me that it is only when you become aware of your transience that you start living life to the fullest. What a paradox. Your inevitable demise draws nearer with every beat of your heart. You know what awaits you. You might even see yourself, laying on your deathbed, counting the last remaining days of your life. Alone. Moments before departing into the eternal darkness. Everyone has to face this, regardless of the life that they have lived. Some people impatiently await their end, while others are terrified of death. The ones that worry me the most belong to a third group. Those who don't think about death. By believing that they will live forever, they take the charm out of this ever fragile life. It only takes a moment for life to end. One moment you're here, the next you're gone. It's this dance of life and death that makes us human. We love life because we fear death. Isn't that the ultimate paradox?

It feels good to read your personal thoughts on a specific matter. I could not have written it better myself. I smiled at the thought.

"What's new?" asked a voice from somewhere within the house.

"Great news! Boris will come out of his coma."

"That's amazing news! And a wonderful surprise! Does it say anything else?"

"No. I haven't been to the hospital yet. I mean, my future self hasn't been to the hospital yet. At the moment, he's sitting at home contemplating life and death."

"Typical."

"Sarcasm doesn't befit you."

"Sarcasm doesn't befit anyone. Which is why it hides behind such an ugly word. Sarcasm. It sounds like something you could pull out of your nose."

I laughed and almost dropped the glass that I was holding.

"I won't buy a new set of crystal just because you break one glass."

"Can't they be bought individually?"

"I don't know. Whatever. It's terrific news for Boris, and you. How are you?"

"I'm not sure. I'm confused. On one hand, I can hardly wait for tomorrow to come, on the other, I'm terrified."

"I can imagine. I'd be scared too if I were in your shoes. Do you want another glass of whiskey? I'll get some wine for me then I'll come out for a cigarette."

"I would love one. Thanks."

Life happens when you start thinking about your imminent death. If that is not absurd, I do not know what is. Of course, there is an elementary logic behind it. It is only once you are aware that you are going to die that you start appreciating life. Perhaps a greater appreciation for the small pleasures in life sprouts up, or you start doing things that you didn't dare to do before. This becomes even truer once you have had a close encounter with death. I have heard numerous stories of how people changed after a near-death experience, which is somewhat logical. A lot of people live their lives in conformity with social norms rather than their wishes. They begin to breathe fully and freely, once they have seen death up close, and it is only after that defining moment that they dare to be who they really are. *He was who he was.* I want this to be inscribed on my tombstone when I die.

CHAPTER FOURTEEN

"There is no tunnel, no fanfares, no virgins. There's only fucking darkness. Darkness and silence. No sounds, no colors, no clouds. Just darkness that extends into eternity."

Boris spoke slower than usual, but he used the same vocabulary as he always did.

"Calm down man. You just woke up from a coma, and I'm already worried you're losing it," I tried to soothe him.

"The only thing I could think about, while I was in this endless darkness, was how I'm going to bust a cap, straight in the head of the fucking bastard who's done this to us."

"I'm sorry about Milena."

He looked through the window as a tear trickled down his cheek.

"I know."

"Can you walk?"

"Of course I can. Do you really think a few bullets could tie me to the bed?"

"Should we go out for a smoke?"

"You've always been a good friend."

While we were smoking behind the hospital, he told me how it all happened. There were two culprits, dressed in black. They were wearing hats, and their faces were hidden behind ski goggles. They entered through the downstairs window or at least Boris assumed that was the case. They made their way into the house in complete silence, climbed up the stairs towards the bedroom. Milena was asleep when they opened the door. Even though Boris was not, it all happened too fast for him to grab hold of the gun that he kept under the bed. The room was filled with barely audible gunshots because of the silencers installed on the killers' weapons. Boris leaped from the bed, but even before he had found his footing, he felt a burning pain radiating through his chest. It was followed - in quick succession - by similar pains in his leg and his back. He dropped to the floor and was instantly submerged in a pitch black darkness from which he only awoke this morning.

"Holy shit," I said. "Horvat knows who did it, but he won't tell me."

"I totally understand. He doesn't want you to flush your career down the drain, too."

"Exactly! Wait a minute. What do you mean mine too?"

"I'll find them."

"Boris, don't be stupid. I know how you feel and ..."

"Bullshit! You don't know how I feel! Can you imagine how you'd feel if you woke up one morning and Sara wasn't there, walking the Earth? How would you feel when you'd find out that you'll never see her again? How can you say that you know how I feel? You have absolutely no idea what I'm going through."

"Boris, listen to me. I know what it's like to lose somebody. Do you remember what I was like when my mother died? Do you?"

"Rok, you know I adored your mom. But you were prepared for her death. You had months to slowly say goodbye to her. You knew that it was going to happen and you pretty much knew when it was going to happen. Milena lay down next to me, kissed me goodnight, which was something she hadn't done in ages, closed her eyes and never opened them again. I'll never forgive myself for not reacting faster, for not grabbing the gun and shooting the fuckers. I'm sure I could have saved her life if I had been faster."

"There was nothing you could've done. They took you by surprise. Nobody could've reacted faster. Nobody. Life isn't a Hollywood movie. You can't always be a hero."

"I should've been one that night. I had the opportunity to do the right thing for once."

"Where is all this coming from? Who put this into your head?"

"You, Mister perfect."

"What?!"

"Yes, you heard it. Your life's a fucking fairy-tale. You've got the perfect girlfriend. Your house is the nicest for miles around. Your …"

"Stop it! How long have we been friends?"

"Twenty years? Twenty-five?"

"Since the first year of primary school. I was with you in third grade when the boys from the seventh grade tried to kick your ass. I was there when you failed your first exam in the fifth grade. I was the one who asked Petra if she wanted to be your girlfriend. Remember? And I made sure you got the answers for your math finals, a subject you always sucked at."

"Of course, I remember all of this."

"I've always been a good friend. I was always there, standing by your side. Have I ever pulled a fast one on you?"

"Not to my knowledge."

"I didn't. Trust me. My life isn't a fairy-tale. I have problems just like everybody else. I struggle from one day to the next. Mainly with myself. And now I have all this diary thing …"

"What diary thing?"

"This will sound really weird, but I swear it's true. I've found a diary on my computer, and it looks like I'm writing it."

"That's not weird! A psychotherapist once suggested I

should keep a diary, so I did for a while. Do you remember when I killed that sixteen-year-old boy who drew a gun during a raid in Medvode?"

"The diary on my computer reveals the next day's events."

"What are you trying to say? It's telling you what is going to happen to you tomorrow? I don't get it."

"It's not me writing it. It's the future me."

"Bullshit."

"I'm telling you the truth. So far everything has happened exactly as it was written."

"That's just crazy!"

"I know."

"How long has this been going on?"

"One week."

Boris remained silent for a few seconds.

"So you knew."

"What?"

"What would happen to me."

"Kind of. But I had no idea at that time what was really happening. I had no idea who was writing it and thought that it was a prank."

Boris jumped on me like a rabid dog. He grabbed me by my neck and pressed me against the wall.

"Fucking bastard! You knew! You knew, and you didn't warn me! How could you?! It's all your fault! It's yours, not mine!"

A security guard came running around the corner, grabbed Boris and pulled him off me. Boris wriggled out of his stranglehold and punched him in the face. The security guard stumbled a few steps backward and radioed for backup.

"Boris, you have to believe me when I tell you there was nothing I could do. I had no idea the diary was about you. If I knew I would have done something, you know that."

"The only thing I know is that Milena would still be

alive if you used that pathetic brain of yours!"

"How could I have known, for fuck's sake?! Imagine you were in my position."

"You try to imagine you're in my position. Fuck off! I mean it Rok, just fuck off! I've had enough of you."

At that moment another three security guards arrived on the scene. Boris did nothing to resist them. He was peacefully escorted back to the hospital. I stood there watching them as they left, and remained motionless even after the automatic doors closed behind them. I realized I had managed to regain and lose my best friend again – all in the same day. Life is a fucking tragedy. One minute, you are harmoniously sitting in the sandpit building sand castles, and then it suddenly starts to rain. You observe how the heavens destroy your magical sculptures, soaked by the cloudburst and in tears because of the destructive heavenly display. This is when you realize life is neither a fairy-tale nor is it fair. You become aware that there is something out there destroying your dreams. Something starts worrying you. You no longer take your happiness for granted, as you discern that your path has lost its innocent simplicity. Your wishes are no longer fulfilled. When was the last time you were happy? How long did it last? A few seconds? A few minutes? What have you learned about happiness? By now, you know it does not last. You know that happiness is measured in fleeting moments. Would it be wrong to be happy all the time? It would be extremely detrimental to world order. Why? Because the best consumers are unhappy. The best voters are unhappy. When you are unhappy, you need something. You need a change. You might be happy when you get a new car, a new job or a new government. Maybe a trip to the Caribbean will make you happy or perhaps a lover, a good book or a movie. But remember, all wishes have something in common. The desire for change. What is wrong with that? What is wrong is that we are looking for changes outside of ourselves rather than trying to change from the inside out, forcing the transformation that we yearn for from within. But why do we need to change? Because we have strayed way off the path as a species. We are magnificent creatures with faulty software. First, we build castles in the sand, and then we pray for rain. Mankind started out as a miracle of nature but has evolved into a natural anomaly. However, Mother nature is very good at returning things to a pure state of equilibrium.

* * *

"He'll calm down and come to his senses," said Sara.

"I'm not so sure about that."

"Try to imagine what he's going through. He's just lost Milena. He's angry at the world. Give him some time."

"I don't understand how he can blame me."

"He's not blaming you, silly. You might have been clumsy with the diary story, but you didn't do anything wrong."

"Exactly. I did nothing wrong. His fate was not in my hands."

"Of course it wasn't. You need to calm down. Here, have a glass of wine. Light a cigarette, relax. You're a bundle of nerves!"

Milena would still be alive if you used that pathetic brain of yours. Boris's words resonated through my mind. I picked up my laptop, and for a moment I imagined the feeling of throwing it against the wall. It did not break the way they do in movies. Instead, it fell to the ground practically unharmed. A fraction of a second later, I was standing next to it, stomping on it angrily. In the end, it gave up under my shoes. I watched it as its plastic and metal intestines spilled across the floor and its robotic life slowly departed. I felt satisfaction. I felt the sweetness of revenge. The next moment I returned to reality and became aware that I had placed the laptop on the spot that was previously occupied by my glass of wine. The glass had remained intact, but its contents were victoriously strutting along a large part of the table. I dashed to the kitchen and grabbed a cloth. While I was cleaning up the spilled wine, my phone rang.

"Hello?"

Silence. I could only hear shallow breaths.

"Who is it?"

I could hear somebody talking in the background, but I could not make out what was being said. It might have just been a TV that was turned on.

"I don't have time for this shit!"

The connection ended. I looked at my screen. A withheld number. I could track it down, but I decided it was most likely nothing more than some kids, screwing around. As kids, we would call up people with last names like Wolf or Butcher or just dial a random number and laugh at our own bright ideas. I put down my telephone and wiped up the remaining wine. I put the cloth in the sink, grabbed the bottle and poured some wine into the glass. I returned to the living room, sat down on the chair and opened my laptop to check if there was a new entry in the diary. There was. Hence, I started reading.

19.45

Boris will be okay. The doctors said that he's a medical miracle. They believe it to be a miracle that he woke up from his coma. They were just about to pull the plug when he suddenly opened his eyes and started to scream uncontrollably…as loud as he could with a tube stuck down his throat. A few hours after he was reborn, we were already smoking behind the hospital building. This is what you do when the universe gives you a second chance. Boris told me what happened or at least his version of events. I could see the anger on his pale face. He didn't cry. He never cried. As I was bidding farewell, I told him we would find the bastards. That I will find them. He nodded and smiled. He said I had always been a good friend. Then he closed his eyes and fell asleep. I have never seen a man fall asleep so quickly. I imagine a near-death experience wears you out. I doubt anyone ever woke up from a coma, jumped out of bed, shouted with joy and ran a marathon. But if something is unbelievable, it doesn't mean it's impossible. Boris has clearly proven this.

I took a sip of the wine. It was a bit too dry for my taste, but I did not really care. The entry I had just read did not mention that Boris and I had had an argument. Not only did we not argue, but we also parted on excellent terms, as best friends. I quickly understood what was happening. The other Rok was not reading the journal from the future, he was the one writing it. The discussion about the unusual diary that mysteriously appeared on my computer never took place. And this meant that there was no argument between Boris and myself like I had experienced a few hours ago. This means that the Rok from the future and I were suddenly living different lives. What would the consequences of this be? Will the new diary entries be entirely different from the fate that awaits me? Is this good or bad? Maybe my life will get back on track, and I will gradually forget about the diary, the past week, the events that I could have changed but did not. Well, one event, if I am precise. An incident I will never be able to forget or change for the better. Regardless of the fact that I had a window into the future, I failed to capitalize on this. I felt like a little schoolboy who had just started reading War and Peace. He knows all the letters and he is a good reader, but he fails to understand what is really written on the pages that he is reading. He tries to imagine the story, but he cannot because his little brain has not experienced enough in life. He soon finds himself in a swimming pool that is too deep, and he can no longer feel the bottom with his feet. Tired of his great desire to prove himself he swims back to the edge, closes the book and returns it to the library the next day. Life is a Ph.D. dissertation read by semi-literate primary school pupils.

I continued reading.

April 1, 2015, 6.45
While sipping black coffee, I was surfing the news web portals. Somebody has won 73 million euros. A large part of Turkey was affected by an electrical blackout. Lufthansa admitted that the pilot on the airplane that crashed into the French Alps last week was suffering from severe depression. A scientific magazine has published the results of research, which shows that parents' income influences the brain complexity of their children. I remembered the study that tried to prove black people were intellectually inferior. Then I started thinking about Boris and what I could have done for this diary to come into your hands sooner. I realized there was nothing I could have done as I only started writing it a day before Boris and Milena were shot. There was nothing you could have done. Try to forget it and look ahead. But whatever you do, don't mention it to Boris.

I reread the last line a thousand times while gasping for air. He knows. This proves that the other Rok knows I am reading his diary. How can this be possible? How can I get in touch with him? Is there a chance of turning this diary into a two-way communication device? For a moment, I stopped thinking. I am reading a diary that I am writing in the future, a parallel universe or wherever, and the thing that I cannot understand is that the other Rok knows I am reading his diary. My thoughts started rushing again. How many Roks are reading this diary? Should I start writing one? Should I try to warn yesterday's Rok not to tell Boris about the diary? I had so many questions and not a single answer that would make any sense. However, as always, there is an absolute truth that encompasses everything that surrounds the diary. There is a single truth that could explain what the hell is going on. A revelation that I am a part of. Unfortunately, I have no idea what is going on. But I know what is going to happen in the near future. Well, I knew, until I made the stupid decision to tell Boris about the damn diary. Causing me to start living a completely different life from the other Rok. And it has gone off the rails. Somehow, I have to let him know that his diary is no longer of any help to me. I have to establish contact. But how do you get in touch with someone from the future?

CHAPTER FIFTEEN

I was sitting in my office, stretched across the chair, staring at the ceiling. Contrary to what the diary stated I did not read the news in the morning. It could have been a conscious decision or the incident with Boris could have drastically separated the future described in the diary from my future. Right then, it did not really matter. It was clear that the other Rok knows I am reading his diary. But he is not aware that our realities are no longer the same. We arrived at a crossroads and went our separate ways. Even if I make peace with Boris soon, which is very unlikely, knowing him like the back of my hand, it would not mean that our paths will merge again. What benefits will I reap from the diary? My thoughts were interrupted by a knock on the door. Tina stepped into the office.

"Rok, Horvat wants to see you."

"Tell him I'll be right there."

"Are you alright?"

"No, but let's not get into it."

"Is there anything I can do to help?"

"No, not this time."

"Okay. But you know where to find me if you need me."

"Thanks."

A few minutes later I was sitting opposite Horvat, pretending to be listening to him.

"… this is an essential operation … it has to be carried

out flawlessly ... orders from the top ... your role is vital ... are you listening to me or are you daydreaming?!"

I was suddenly back in the office.

"Err, yes, I'm listening. I agree."

"Agree with what?"

"I will take part in the operation."

"That wasn't a suggestion! Did you think you had a choice? It was an order, do you understand?! An order! Grab a coffee, wake up, stop daydreaming and start working. Tick tock, time is your enemy."

"Will that be all?"

"Here is everything you need to know about the case. You will report directly to Nolan. Of course, I also need to be informed how the case is progressing, so drop by my office every now and then."

"Understood."

I grabbed the folder with the documents that was lying on Horvat's desk and stormed out of the office. I decided to take his advice and get some air. I had to clear my head. I had to stop thinking about the diary. But how can you stop thinking about something that is so strange and exciting?

"Do you want to grab a coffee?" asked Tina.

"How did you know what was on my mind?"

"Should we go together?"

"Of course."

I wasn't trying to be polite. I actually wanted a bit of company. It would make it easier to think about something else.

"Should we go to STA?"

"Sure."

"Wait a minute, I just need to use the restroom. I'll be right back."

"No worries. Take your time."

"Two minutes."

"I'll wait outside."

* * *

Seven minutes later, we were sitting in the bar's garden. The spring sun was warm, and we were talking about unimportant things.

"It's unbelievable. I would expect it from someone else, but not from Alen."

"I always thought he was a quiet one, so I'm not really surprised," I said.

"Surely you don't think this is normal."

"What is normal these days? Some people think it's normal to have piercings in their scrotums, while other people think it's normal to spend their holidays in the same caravan year after year. Alen obviously thinks it's normal to show his dick off on a first date."

"That's not the real problem. We're all grown-ups, first dates are different than they were when we were young. What shocked me was that Alen pulled it out while he was driving."

"I bet you liked it."

"It seemed like he was showing off. Hey, look at my big dick and bam, suddenly it was out there, in plain view."

"And?"

"What do you mean and? I told him to put it back where it came from and that he had lost any chance he might have had with me. I'm not easy nor stupid. He kept insisting that I'd hold it for a while and kept repeating that he likes me. The dick, not him. That his dick likes me. Well, that was just a step too far."

I could barely contain my laughter.

"When he dropped me off at home, he said he had a great time and asked me if I had a good time too. As if nothing had ever happened! As if he hadn't been driving down the street, five minutes before, with his dick on the steering wheel! People are sick, Rok, even when they seem to be innocent geeks on the surface, they have - in reality –

sick, twisted minds."

"Or maybe because of it."

"Because they're geeks? I guess that's possible. Like you said before, it's always the silent ones."

"Have you spoken to Boris?" I asked.

"I visited him yesterday afternoon. Why?"

"Just asking."

"I can't believe he made such an excellent recovery. A few days ago the doctors were writing him off."

"Did you know they were about to pull the plug when he woke up?"

"No. Who told you that?"

"I spoke to the doctors."

"Unbelievable, that really is fighting to the very end."

"I hope he won't do anything stupid," I said.

"What do you mean?"

"Think about it. What would you do if you were in Boris's shoes?"

"Ah, now I get you. I hope he won't do it."

"You know him. He won't just forget about it. He loved Milena way too much. And he has a gigantic ego that won't allow anyone to solve this case without him."

"Do you think he'll do it on his own? Horvat would never let him."

"What can he do? He won't put him on the case, and he'll try to block all communication channels, but Boris is not stupid. He has his own sources, he knows people on the street. If he wants to get to the bottom of it, he will."

"Are you going to help him?"

"I don't think so."

"He'll be disappointed."

"I think he already is."

"What do you mean? Have you spoken to him about this?"

"No. Not about this."

"What then? I mean, if you don't want to talk about it, I won't push you. We can change the subject."

I had to tell somebody. I raised the cup of coffee and took a sip. Then I took a cigarette out of the box and slowly brought it to my mouth. I lit it up, inhaled, blew the smoke from my lungs and looked deep into Tina's eyes.

"Do you remember the diary I told you about last time we met in Prulček?"

"Of course I do. I've wanted to ask you about it ever since. What happened? Did forensics find anything?"

"Yes."

Tina also lit a fresh cigarette.

"Don't breathe a word of this to anybody. This is strictly between you and me. Do you understand?"

She nodded. I trusted her. She would not screw me over.

"The diary is not writing itself, and it isn't being written by somebody else. The simplest explanation is, without going into too many theories and assumptions, that it's me who's writing the diary in the future or some sort of parallel universe."

I could see that I had captured her interest. Who would not be interested in a story like this? She was listening with her eyes wide open and slightly parted lips. She only closed her mouth when she wrapped her lips around the cigarette. I did not go into too much detail and I did not explain the contents of the diary. Of course, I did have to tell her the bits and pieces that were vital to the story.

"You knew Boris would get shot?"

"I did. But at the time, I had no idea what I was reading. I didn't know that it was about him, I didn't even know it was about me. It wasn't until the next day that I realized what was happening and by then it was too late. How could I've known? What could I've done?"

"Nothing. You've done everything you could. Don't overthink it, Rok. The past can't be changed."

Bam. The past can't be changed. Damn! I leaped to Tina and kissed her on her mouth.

"Hey! What's happening?"

"I have to go and do something!"

"You haven't even finished your coffee. Okay, go. I'll pay for the coffees."

I ran down the stairs and called a taxi. It would only take me about twenty minutes to walk home. I also had a car parked nearby, but I did not want to waste any time. This was too important. What you are, I was. What I am, you will be. The solution had been right in front of my eyes the whole time, but I had not noticed it. I had to get hold of my laptop as quickly as possible.

* * *

I had no idea whether the plan would work, but it was worth a shot. The logic behind it was simple. If the Rok from the future can communicate with me through my laptop, then there is a chance that I can establish contact with Rok or several Roks from the past. It was worth giving it a try. I didn't have anything to lose. If it worked, I could do something big and important. I opened the Word document and started writing.

April 1, 2015, Wednesday
This is not an April Fools' prank. Nobody is trying to mess with you, and your computer has not been hacked. I am Rok Kopitar, and this is my first attempt at establishing contact with you. That is, me in the past. I know it sounds crazy, but believe me, this is real.

I stopped writing and paused for thought. What am I doing? There are two possibilities. The Rok from the past is either reading the same diary and he most likely made the same mistake I did, or he is not reading it and he never got into an argument with Boris. The idea that I thought was fantastic just half an hour ago, suddenly seemed more of a burden than a solution. What did I want to achieve?

The answer was clear. I wanted my life to return to its regular path. I aspired to wipe out all the events that had happened during the past week. I needed to wake up from this dream that was slowly turning into a nightmare. I was in desperate need of a drink and some time to think. I moved to the terrace with a glass in one hand and a cigarette in the other. That is where I get my best ideas. It is my temple. I took a long swig of whiskey, flexed my brain cells and started connecting my dispersed thoughts. It only took a few seconds - or at least that is how it seemed - for an idea to start emerging. So far, I have not found a way to communicate with the Rok from the future, and I find it hard to imagine that this will ever be possible. My future is being created as I go along and it has not taken place yet, even though I know how it unravels. I have already learned that I can behave differently than what is described in the diary, but with this, I only move further away from the future that was outlined. This happened when I told Boris about the diary. What would have happened if I had not told him? What if there is a present time where I had not mentioned the journal to Boris and where we are still friends? Of course, it has to exist. I remember I had read that time is not linear, but until this moment, I had not really dwelled on the meaning of it. Life is made of decisions. These decisions can be trivial or significant, but each decision leads to an alternate reality. I took another sip while my brain was humming like crazy. It seemed logical to conclude that there are not merely two Roks, the one from the future and me. I remembered the dream I had a few days ago. *We come in infinite numbers, and there were ever more of us.* If there is a Rok who lives one day in the future, there is also a Rok who lives two days in the future. And so forth. And back. Somewhere, or at some time, there is a Rok Kopitar who is lying on his deathbed. And of course, there is a Rok Kopitar who has just been born. *We come in infinite numbers.* But this was not the essential determination of my contemplation on life. If time is not linear and if endless realities genuinely exist, this can only mean one thing. It is what people have unsuccessfully been searching for and remain searching for to this day. It is the Holy Grail. On April 1, 2015, on April Fools' Day, I realized that life is, in fact, the most celebrated joke of all. Maybe it could be best described as a large theater where innumerable repetitions of innumerable performances are being performed on innumerable stages. Every recurrence differs slightly and has a slight change in the cast. I know it sounds complicated and it is hard to explain, but in its essence, it is perfectly simple. We are all going to die, but, at the same time, all of us will live forever. I raised the glass and drank the last few drops of whiskey. I looked at the sky, and for a moment, it felt as if I could feel every single cell in my body. I felt connected to my surroundings. To everything that surrounded me. It was an unusual feeling of bliss. Total calmness. At that moment I knew that everything was exactly as it was supposed to be. Nothing was neither right nor wrong. Every action was influential, although time had no essential meaning. We exist, and we do not at the same time. One and zero. I stood up and remained standing proudly in the center of the terrace. Maybe a minute had passed, perhaps more, conceivably it might have even been an eternity. Life's soundtrack was muted, the images around me had blurred, thoughts had vanished. I sank into darkness and silence, contemplating my immortality.

CHAPTER SIXTEEN

"Are you okay, Rok?"

Sara's voice woke me up.

"Eh? Where am I?"

"On the sofa, in the living room."

"How long was I asleep?"

"I have no idea, I just returned home."

"What's the time?"

"Ten past five."

It felt as if I had slept for more than five hours.

"Were you at work?"

"I was, but I rushed back home after a crazy idea popped into my head."

"What sort of an idea?"

"Do you want to go out and grab a bite?"

"Should we go to Trta?"

"Sounds great!"

Ten minutes later, we were sitting in the garden of the pizzeria in Prule, staring at the menu.

"Are you ready to order? What can I get you to drink?"

"I'll have a Human Fish ale," Sara responded with no hesitation.

"I'll have a Radler."

"Grapefruit flavor?"

"Yes please."

"And what would you like to eat? Or do you need more time to decide?"

"I'll have a Trevisiana pizza with an egg," Sara said

immediately.

"I'll have the Farmer's Delight."

"Do you want an eggsy on top?"

I looked at the young waiter.

"No, I will not have an eggsy, thank you."

"Thank you."

He rushed inside. I lit up a cigarette and looked at Sara.

"What's bothering you?" she asked.

"I don't know how to tell you this, but I had a crazy epiphany today."

"Really? What was it?"

"I'm not sure I know how to tell you."

"I'm not stupid. You know you can tell me anything. If there's something, which I don't understand, I'll just have to ask you to elaborate a bit."

"Okay, here it is. Today I had this idea that I should write a diary to myself in the past. You know, like Rok from the future is writing to me."

"That sounds like a pretty logical idea. And? What did you write?"

"I wrote down a few sentences, and then I realized that it was highly unlikely to change anything."

"Because the Rok from the past might be reading the same diary?"

I adored this woman's intelligence.

"Exactly! If I can read it, then all the Roks following me can read it too. If they can't read it, they're just living their lives as if nothing unusual has happened."

She listened attentively and waited for me to continue.

"Last night I got the final confirmation that he knows I'm reading what he's writing. He wrote directly to me. Or to us, if there are more of us who can read it."

"What did he write?"

"He wrote that I shouldn't tell Boris. There was nothing that I could do about the shooting. That he only started writing the diary one day before the shooting."

"Interesting."

"I agree. But I've already told Boris, and by doing so, I've changed the course of events. The future me is on a different path than the present me. I have no use for the diary anymore."

"That is not necessarily true."

"What do you mean?"

"Even if you've currently changed the course of events with a single action, it's still possible that your paths will meet again. Look at it as a detour. You've turned off the main road, but at some point, you'll be back on it. If I were you, I'd wait and see what happens."

"Let me get back to my thought. I was trying to understand what happens in parallel lives, in the lives of the Roks before me and all those to come. If there are two Roks, there has to be an endless number of us. Endless. In the future, in the past and in the present …"

"A Human Fish for the young lady and a Radler for you, sir."

"Thank you."

I waited for the waiter to disappear.

"Go on," said Sara.

"So, there are endless Roks and endless Saras and infinite versions of all the people who are currently living or who have ever lived on Earth. And countless versions of the people who are still to come. Time is not linear; we don't live from birth to death. Every time we make a decision, a number of new realities are created, some parallel lives emerge, each taking its own course. There's my time, your time, the waiter's time. There's a time where I ordered a pizza with pancetta instead of the Farmer's Delight, a time where you ordered a Coca-Cola instead of a beer and a time where you decided that we should go to Trnovski Zvon instead of Trta. Every decision takes us down a different path, but that doesn't mean that all the other paths cease to exist. Whenever we reach a decision, one or more parallel lives are created, one for each of the possible scenarios."

"Uff, I think I need something stronger than beer."

She laughed.

"Do you think I'm going crazy?"

"I think anyone who would start thinking about what you're thinking about would go crazy. I don't think our brains can understand the scope of what you're saying. How many people have lived on Earth so far? Fifty billion? One hundred billion?"

"I would say more than one hundred billion."

"It really doesn't matter whether there were one hundred billion or one. Infinite versions of one man are still infinite."

The waiter brought our pizzas.

"Trevisiana with an eggsy for the young lady and a Farmer's Delight for you, sir."

"Could we have two Jamesons on the rocks?" asked Sara.

"Of course, miss. Anything for you sir?"

He laughed at his own clever response.

"Yes, I'll also have two on the rocks."

Sara laughed.

"So four Jamesons on the rocks?"

He looked doubtfully at Sara.

"That will do for starters," she replied.

"I'll bring them straight away."

I cut into the pizza. It was only now when I had it in front of me that I realized how hungry I really was.

"Where were we?" I asked with a full mouth.

"That infinite is infinite, no matter what number you multiply it by."

"That's true. But two infinities are still twice as much as a single infinity."

"Infinity is infinity, eternity is eternity. If something is eternal there cannot be something more eternal."

"Hmm."

"Four Jamesons for the young lady."

It seems some people take April Fool's Day too literally.

"Thank you," said Sara. "You've truly taken the spirit of this day to heart, haven't you?"

"I'm trying to keep up a relaxed atmosphere. Where would we be if there was no fun in life?"

He walked up to the young couple who had just sat two tables away, with his head held high.

"Are you paying with student coupons?" I could hear him ask before I refocused on our discussion.

"If I understand you correctly, you're saying that there is a certain number of people living on this planet and they all have an infinite number of versions. However, in reality, it doesn't matter if there was a single man as infinite is infinite regardless of what number we multiply it by."

"Yes, that's the gist of it," Sara confirmed.

"That's crazy. Do you realize what this means?"

"What?"

"That all of human history, the entire history of our planet, the universe, everything that exists and does not exist, exists at the same time."

"That's right."

I took a sip of Jameson. I looked at the plate in front of me. I was not even aware I had already finished half of my pizza. This discussion was crazy. But it was no more insane than the fact that my computer was giving me insight into another dimension, into my life in a parallel universe, into the future. Some people would kill to have this opportunity, maybe they even have. It would be much too egocentric to think that I am the only person in the world who has or has had a window into a second life. Jules Verne wrote about submarines, traveling to the Moon and to the center of the Earth. It is possible that he merely had a vivid imagination, but it is also possible that he could peek into the future. Not to mention Nostradamus, he obviously had some remarkably accurate predictions. I read somewhere that they found a plaque in his tomb that correctly predicted the day it would be opened. I remembered the YouTube videos that Sara and I watched a few months ago. The videos were recorded fifty years ago, and yet they showed people with cell phones. In some of them, people suddenly appeared and disappeared. Of course, it is possible that these were just clever montages, but if I take into account everything I have realized today and the current debate I am having with Sara, I would say that at least some of the videos must be genuine and show people traveling through time. If the Rok from the future discovered a way to communicate with the past, then there must be a way to physically travel through time. But how?

"Where has your mind wandered off to?" Sara broke my line of thought.

"Hey, I just remembered. Is it okay for you to be drinking alcohol?"

"Just this week and then I'll stop. The same goes for smoking."

"Okay. I was thinking about time travel. Do you remember the videos we recently watched?"

"Yes."

"Well, I believe them now."

"Anything is possible."

"No matter how crazy it appears to be?"

"Is it crazier than an infinite number of universes?"

I laughed. I truly love this woman. If I were explaining this to anyone else, he or she would have thought that I had lost it, but she is just sitting here, eating her pizza, drinking whiskey and talking about parallel universes, infinite lives, and time travel. Screw the complexity of life and the universe. Screw the tremendous number of possibilities. Moments like these are what really counts. People with an open mind, people who are able to think with their own heads, they are the ones who matter. No changes have ever come from people blindly following well-established dogmas.

"I've decided to get to the bottom of this," I said.

"How?"

"I'm not sure yet. But reaching a decision is always the first step."

"That's the spirit! How can I help you?"

"You are helping me already. Just by believing I'm not a total idiot."

"I'm actually rather fond of idiots. Do you want a slice of my pizza?"

"You know I don't like arugula."

"Ah, so I'm still with the same Rok."

Her lips spread into a broad smile.

"Which Rok?"

We both laughed out loud at the same time. Life happens when you realize you have bumped into a person who is willing to accept you exactly as you are and who is prepared to openly discuss things that normal ears and brains would consider utterly incomprehensible and stupid. Just because we do not understand something, it does not mean that it is impossible. Numerous individuals have been ridiculed throughout history, and unfortunately a lot of them struggled because of this. But some ignored the ridicule. They persisted in their beliefs and achieved what they set out to accomplish. Who knows where we would be today if everybody gave up because they were ridiculed by the rest of society. Or where we would be if all of the great and original thinkers were accepted and aided by the community. Life is like a sailboat. The direction of travel depends on the wind and the currents. Some remain on the open seas forever, others reach land. However, what worries me is that most people never even get on board.

* * *

Sara and I got home around eight in the evening, and we continued our conversation over a glass of Chardonnay. Of course, I checked the diary before we sat down to continue our discussion, but there were no new entries.

"I'm going to repeat what I've always believed. If something is incredible, it doesn't mean that it's impossible," said Sara.

"I know. Anything is possible."

"I only wanted to say that our minds find it hard to imagine things, which they've never experienced, seen, read or heard. On the other hand, we have accepted certain scientific assumptions as absolute truths, and we don't even question them anymore. In reality, we've become lazy creatures as far as thinking goes."

"I find it hard to imagine a universe or universes where time doesn't exist and where endless possibilities exist. The more I think about it, the less I understand," I said.

"Of course. Take the big bang, the beginning of the universe, for instance. It's generally believed that the universe and everything within it emerged from nothing or a tiny point that contained infinite amount of energy. Which developed into the infinite universe in an infinitely short period of time."

"And what do you think about that?"

"I think it's all crap."

"Even bigger crap than the idea that the universe was created by an old man with a beard?"

Sara laughed.

"Yes, it's even bigger crap than that. Well, now that you mentioned creationism, we have two accepted truths that share a common point. Both theories believe that everything was created from nothing. In the first theory, the universe was brought into being by an unknown phenomenon, while in the other it was started by an unknown highly developed being. In my opinion, they are both highly unlikely. Especially if we consider the fact that energy can't emerge from nothing and can't disappear into nothing."

"Didn't Einstein write about this?" I asked.

"Amongst others. This is the first law of thermodynamics. The total energy in a sealed system, which the universe is, is constant. It can only change from one form to another."

"Hmmm. But how can we apply this law to our theory of parallel universes, where the realities are created as we go along? At every crossroad, you become multiple versions of yourself and all of them exist in the physical world."

"If they've all existed from the very beginning, then they don't appear from nothing. Appear is the right word only if we assume time is linear. Something that previously didn't exist now exists. But we've already ascertained that time isn't linear, and we have the proof of this in your diary."

"Ufff. This is still uncharted territory. I can't even begin to imagine the things we're talking about."

"Can you imagine how small a proton is?"

"No," I admitted.

"See. There's no way we'll solve the issues of parallel universes and the simultaneous existence of all realities today. We don't even know if anyone will ever discover the absolute truth. As I said, our minds have certain limitations."

"I think our minds — I mean our two minds - are extremely open to new theories."

"That's why I love you. You never accept or reject an idea just because you read it somewhere."

"I've always been a skeptic. I always liked to think with my own head. In school, they always used to say I disrupted the lessons by constantly raising my hand, but I believe that questioning leads to progress."

"Questioning and the desire to understand."

"And not the thirst for knowledge?"

"Or the desire to get good marks."

"I read that Einstein had problems with physics in school," I said.

"Nobody likes a smartass."

"I would rather assume that nobody likes free spirits. Our society tries to shape us all from the same mold. Although the outline of the design doesn't fit us all, it's forced upon us. And it's always ill-conceived when someone ventures outside of the pre-conceived box. We swallow the truths that are served to us on silver platters. The more we keep filling our heads with knowledge, the emptier we become."

"But those who reject the silver platter, those who aren't afraid to stand out, are highly respected. It's not the fault of the educational system that people want to be apathetic and malleable."

"But the educational system is a part of a larger system that wants people to be exactly like that. That's why it expels all individuals who dare to think beyond the prescribed framework."

"There's nothing wrong with our exile."

I smiled.

"You're right."

"Was there anything new in the diary?" Sara asked.

"There was nothing new twenty minutes ago."

"Want to watch a documentary?"

"Of course I do."

"Dinner, drinks and this conversation have worn me out".

"What if we finally watched Interstellar?"

"Great idea! Will you download it while I take a quick shower?"

"Or even better, let's take a shower together while the movie is downloading."

"I was wondering if you'd suggest that. See you in the bathroom."

"Be right there."

CHAPTER SEVENTEEN

It was four-fifteen in the morning, and I was pouring coffee into the cup. It was still dark outside, but that was one of the things I liked about early mornings. The darkness and the silence. It made me think of Boris's near death experience. Less than forty-eight hours had passed since our argument, but it seemed like an eternity to me. Sara is convinced he will reconsider what has happened and that we will be friends again, but I am not so sure. Boris is a good man, but when he is got something stuck in his head, it is hard to move him. I have never known a more stubborn man. But because life is full of surprises and because I believe anything is possible, I trust that there is a possibility that he will call me, however small that chance may be. I love the smell of coffee first thing in the morning. The aroma wakes me up before I even try to open my eyes.

I sat at the table with the hot enticing liquid in my cup and brought my laptop to life. There were no new entries in the diary. I reread the last entry again. There was nothing you could have done. Try to forget it and look ahead. "I am looking ahead," I said to the screen in a whisper. "I'm looking ahead but I can't see." I knew what was going to happen, but this knowledge was of no help to me. In fact, it was doing the opposite, it was harming me. What is the point of having insight into the future? While I was dealing with more or less paranormal questions, I heard a quiet but recognizable noise. Somebody wanted to chat with me on Facebook. I clicked on the appropriate tab, looked at the bottom right corner of the screen and read the name. Wet Dreams Katka. Who the fuck is that?!

"Hi, Rok. Are you having trouble sleeping too?"

"Who are you?"

"What do you mean, who am I? Don't you remember me?"

"I honestly have no idea."

I got no response for about thirty seconds, maybe a bit more. In the meantime, I unsuccessfully scanned her profile for a recognizable photograph, but all the profile photos were either of cats or dogs or positive statements borrowed from the internet. However, what followed was very graspable.

"Do you remember me now?"

I was staring at a photograph of big breasts, and I tried to decipher who they belonged to.

"Martina?"

"You're kidding, right?"

"Unfortunately not. If you're not Martina, I have no idea who you are."

Wet Dreams Katka subjected me to another medium length virtual silence. I looked at the pair in the photograph again trying to find a recognizable detail that would help me recall their owner. Before I was able to initiate my in-depth research, I had the feeling that somebody was standing behind me.

"Nice boobs. So this is why you get up so early?"

I turned around and saw Sara with a glass of water in her hands.

"I honestly have no idea what's going on."

"You don't need to come up with excuses. You're a man. It's all normal stuff."

"No, I honestly have no idea who sent me these."

"Listen, I'm going back to bed. You do what you have to. Really, there is nothing wrong with it."

She kissed me and walked back towards the bedroom. I watched her for a few seconds as she left the room, and then I went back to my research. New photographs were waiting for me. This time Katka, who could for all I know be a psychopath with acne so bad that it served her as a universal and cheap contraceptive, offered me a glimpse of the most intimate part of her body.

"Well?"

"Maybe it would be easier if you sent me a photograph of your face."

"It might be easier, but it certainly wouldn't be as fun."

"I have neither the time nor the will for this sort of stuff. I won't send you a photo of my dick. I won't try guessing who you are from photographs of boobs and a cunt that you could've snatched from the internet. As far as I'm concerned, we're done unless you tell me who you are and what your excuse is for pestering me at four thirty in the morning."

"You're so boring."

"I know. But I'm convinced there are plenty of guys who are up at this time of the morning and would do anything to have a conversation like this."

"Maybe, but they're not you, are they?"

"And what makes me so special?"

"Ten years ago you didn't do what every other man would've done."

I took a sip of coffee and went on a journey through time, in search of the past, in my mind. I looked at the photographs once again.

"Katarina?"

"Finally!"

"How are you? Where have you been?"

"I'm okay. I've been living in Toronto for the past six years."

"That's good news. So you managed to get there eventually."

"I did, and it's fantastic. You know I love big cities. And Canada is a wonderful country, I feel much more at home here than I ever did in Slovenia."

"I can imagine. What made you think of me?"

"I often think of you. How's life treating you?"

"Same old, same old."

"I see you've managed to become a detective, just like you always wanted."

"Well, there was a time when I wanted to study pandas."

"Haha. Do you still see Boris?"

I took a little break for a sip of coffee. I needed to figure out what direction I wanted to lead this conversation into. She does not need to know everything. I also had no proof it really was Katarina on the other side of this chat. Photographs or not, in the mysterious virtual world you always need to use a bit of common sense and be on your toes.

"Yeah, we work together."

"Oh, that's great. How's he doing?"

"He's okay. He's still grumpy."

"I'm glad you two remained friends. I remember you were inseparable."

"We still are."

"That's nice."

It seemed I was actually talking to Katarina. However, somebody else could be reading our conversation.

"Do you ever come back to Slovenia?"

"I'll come in the summer for a week or so, to see my family and friends. If you give me your number, I'll call you, and we can get together for a coffee. If you want to, of course."

"I'd love to. 045 667 558. Can you give me yours? I

don't answer numbers I don't recognize."

"Haha. I know. You always did that. My number is +1 416 788 1516."

"Thank you. I'll see you this summer then. Btw, your tits have grown."

"LOL. Silly thing. It comes with age. And with a leisurely lifestyle. Take care and look after Sara."

I needed a few seconds.

"How do you know about Sara?"

A virtual breeze.

"Katarina?"

Nothing. No reply. Okay, calm down. She must have spoken to a mutual acquaintance who told her about Sara and me. That is not unusual, people talk. And I have her telephone number, which I can check anytime. I read the entire conversation through once more. I had not let anything slip that I should not have. I concluded I was being unnecessarily paranoid. I grabbed the half-empty cup and stepped outside to get some fresh air. I lit a cigarette and tried not to think about what had just happened. Ten minutes later, I decided that one coffee was not enough, so I boiled some water and put two spoonfuls of instant coffee into the cup. I always make my first early morning coffee with the stovetop coffee maker, but all the ones that follow are instant, from a machine or a bar. Depending on where I am when a sudden craving for caffeine overrides my mind. I usually drink between four and seven coffees a day, and I smoke about twenty cigarettes. I am not a good example of a man living a healthy lifestyle, but I have never been seriously ill. Life is a Russian roulette. We are constantly pulling the trigger without thinking there might be a bullet in the gun. But there is a bullet for everyone, ready to pierce our brains. It might hit tomorrow, it might be half an eternity away. Life is a game of Russian roulette, and there are no winners.

CHAPTER EIGHTEEN

I was supposed to meet up with Nolan at eight, but his secretary called and moved the meeting by an hour. I skimmed through the materials given to me by Horvat. Orion Pax was a complicated operation that was being implemented across eight countries. The goal of the Slovene team, which consisted of me and six others, was to obtain as much information as possible on Walter. I knew that the quickest way to gain this information was by questioning Kolya. But usually, the swiftest way is not the easiest. At this point, Kolya had been in custody for one week, and we had conducted four lengthy interviews with him. So far, he had revealed nothing. Sometimes I wish I worked for the American military. Then I could pull the information out of the bastard along with his teeth. I decided to use more refined tactics. I called the police station on Trdinova and announced that I would hold an interrogation at ten thirty. I had half an hour to kill until my meeting with Nolan and the caffeine levels in my blood were drastically low, so I decided to grab a coffee from the place across the road.

It was pleasant outside; the weather was very unusual for April. The sun was shining, and it was fifteen degrees. I sat at a table in the Pelican's garden. A few seconds later Mirela, the waitress, came hovering by.

"Hi, Rok! You're early today. Coffee with milk?"

"Yes, please. And a glass of fresh orange juice."

"I'll bring it straight away."

The tables around me were empty. An old lady was sitting on the other side of the garden, in the corner, taking short sips of her cappuccino. I smiled at her when she looked at me for a moment, but she failed to return the smile or acknowledge me in any other way.

"There you go, coffee with milk and a fresh orange juice. I was quick because I know you're in a hurry."

I leaned closer towards her.

"Mirela, you truly are a star."

She giggled and winked at me.

"You know I'm always willing to go the extra mile for you."

"Which is why you are my favorite waitress," I lied.

She blushed.

"And you are my favorite client. Not to mention the most handsome one too."

Another wink, this time slightly more spontaneous, before she rushed inside.

I lit a cigarette and stared at the Ministry of internal affairs' building where we had our offices. We called it headquarters. Sometimes we called it the nest depending on the context and the people we were talking to. I have been working for the investigation department for almost five years now; I joined as soon as I finished my studies. I did not have any grand ambitions; I liked my current position. Besides, a higher rank brings greater responsibility and additional stress. Of course, it also comes with a more alluring office and a higher salary, but I really enjoyed being an operative. I loved fieldwork. I loved feeling useful. My superiors knew this and respected it. But they mainly felt comfortable knowing that they did not have to worry that I would be after their comfy leather chairs, which created a fine, firm basis for cooperation.

Suddenly my thoughts were disturbed by a trembling female voice.

"Do you have a light, young sir?"

I looked up. It was the woman from the far corner. She was about seventy years old, maybe a bit more, but certainly no less.

"Of course," I replied as I handed her the lighter.

It lit up on the second attempt. The lady inhaled and blew out the first puff of smoke. Old school, I thought, as she took a deep breath and sighed while exhaling.

"This is my first cigarette in thirty-two years, you know. My husband left me today."

Apparently, she was waiting for me to ask what had happened, but I did not. I waited for her to continue with her story at her own pace. Old ladies always have more to say.

"He found another woman. She's twenty years younger. After fifty-five years of marriage."

I made some quick calculations in my mind. She must have been very young when she got married.

"He never cheated on me. He didn't cheat now either. He just told me he was leaving. And he did."

"Are you celebrating or grieving?" I finally asked her. She started laughing out loud.

"Oh, young man, how old are you? Thirty?"

"Close enough."

"My husband is a good man you know, they don't make them like that anymore. But he is also dead boring. I beg you, choose a woman with whom you'll have something to talk to about thirty years down the line. I gave up after ten. And I was only twenty-seven years old at the time."

"Why didn't you file for a divorce sooner?"

She sat down on the chair opposite me.

"Things used to be different, you know. Today's youth gets married and divorced before you can say sexual intercourse."

"You mean hungry like a horse? Before you can say hungry like a horse."

"I know what I said. Sexual intercourse. I know what you're thinking. It's inappropriate for an old woman like me to talk about sex. My husband might not have given it to me enough over the past few years, but now I'm free, and I can find myself some young meat."

"I'm sure you won't find it hard to find someone. I would've never guessed that you were a day over fifty."

"You're sweet. My husband is too. But incredibly boring."

"I know, you already mentioned it. Well, I wish you all the best in your quest for young meat. Unfortunately, I have to bid you farewell, work awaits."

"Where do you work?"

"I serve the country, madam."

I drank what was left of the orange juice and left three euros on the table.

"Have a lovely day madam. Don't overdo it on the smoking. Your lungs are no longer used to the cigarette smoke."

"These lungs have been through two wars! Where has the waitress gone to? I need a real drink."

As I was leaving towards the headquarters, Mirela waved from behind the bar. I winked at her and moments after I almost got run over by a lunatic, who ran a red light, while I was crossing the road. Russian roulette.

* * *

"It is absolutely essential that we get as much information as possible from Kolya," said Nolan.

"I know, but he isn't a big talker, and we don't have any real leverage. There's nothing we can pin on him. We have no substantial evidence."

"Find it. This should be your number one priority. We have to reach Walter. Do you understand?"

"Yes, we'll try our best."

"I don't believe I need to stress that this could be extremely beneficial to your careers."

And for his. He couldn't afford to have another black mark on his record.

"I understand. We'll get down to work immediately. I plan to interrogate Kolya at ten thirty. I'll let you know how it goes."

"Please do. If you need any help, I am at your disposal. Talk to you soon."

He hung up. I remained calm even though I was aware of the seriousness of the situation. I had no idea how I would conduct the cross-examination, but that was not unusual for me. I was good at improvising, and that was important. Interrogations are like life. You can be prepared for all possible scenarios, but sooner or later you will come across a situation in which you will have to react instantly. Nobody can prepare you for these turning points, nobody can make a decision instead of you. The ability to improvise is a significant human characteristic.

* * *

It was ten twenty, and I was standing in front of the police station on Trdinova smoking a cigarette and drinking a revolting coffee from the coffee machine. A policeman I did not know stood next to me. Green. Coincidentally, this also happened to be his last name.

"I am curious to see whether you'll manage to squeeze anything out of him," he said.

"So am I."

I gave him a forced smile. I was not in the mood to chat.

"How is it up there? In headquarters?"

"It's nice."

"I hope I'll work up there one day. That's where all the real action is."

"True, there's always action up there."

I put out my cigarette and wished Green a nice day. I entered the station and waved to the policeman behind the counter. He replied to the greeting and gestured that I should enter the interrogation room. Kolya was already sitting behind the table. I entered the room and sat down opposite him. We looked at each other for a few seconds, and then he started talking.

"I see that they've brought a suit in."

I never wore a suit. I always wore a sports jacket over a T-Shirt. But I knew what he meant.

"They always call in the suits for the big criminals. You should know that by now."

"Big criminals? I am an honest citizen, I pay taxes and everything."

"The state gets nothing from you dealing coke."

"What are you talking about? Coke? Are you insane?"

"You can end the charades Kolya. We both know what this is all about. If you cooperate, we will let you off easy. You'll serve a few years, but we'll make sure you celebrate your fortieth with your friends on the outside. So be smart and tell us what we want to know."

"And what exactly do you want to know?"

"We want to find Walter."

Kolya stared at me for a few moments, and then he started laughing uncontrollably as if I had just rattled off the best joke in the world.

"I'm glad you find this amusing."

He was still laughing like a moron. I wanted to push my fist down his throat and rip out his tonsils.

"I don't know anybody called Walter."

"Of course you do. I just need to rattle that pea-sized brain of yours."

"Did you know I took an IQ test?"

"Only to find out you didn't need a test to tell you that you're an idiot?"

"I have an IQ of 175."

"Oh, c'mon. I heard Matt Damon has 160."

"Matt Damon is dumb!"

"Then that tells you everything you need to know about those tests. Are you going to answer my question or not?"

"I already have."

I signaled the policeman at the door to leave the interrogation room. I had no idea who was on Walter's payroll.

"Have we reached the point where you kick the crap out of me?" he asked, still smiling.

"Listen to me. I know you know where Walter is. I also know you're not stupid enough to rat him out like that. We can offer you protection. We can send you somewhere where Walter and his pals will never find you. We can give you a new life. How much have you managed to grab for yourself during the years you've been working for him? Three million, five perhaps? Wouldn't it be great to spend all that money on an island in paradise, without worrying that anyone is coming for you? Think about it."

He suddenly became serious. He was definitely considering my offer. He joined his hands in front of his mouth and looked straight into my eyes. I have got him, I thought.

"I've always wanted to live in Cuba," he finally said.

"Good choice. I've heard it's dead cheap there."

"And the Cubans are also dead cheap."

"Rum, cigars, salsa, beautiful women. I want you to be happy."

"Unfortunately, I can't tell you something I don't know."

"You can lead me to Zoran. We will continue from there."

"The only Zoran I know is sitting in a comfy leather chair at city hall."

"Would you prefer a small prison cell?"

"It's not about what I prefer. It's about wanting to live."

"Prison is no life."

"Neither is a coffin."

"I promise that we can protect you."

"You don't know these people you're looking for. You've got no idea what they're capable of and what you're getting yourself into."

"Well, why don't you tell me then."

"Let's put it like this. If I tell you anything, my corpse will be found before you lay down next to your beautiful girlfriend tonight. The official explanation would be that I hung myself or that I slashed my wrists with a razor blade that I somehow managed to smuggle past the policemen. No Cuba. They would take me out the second they hear that I ratted them out. I wouldn't get to sign my confession, let alone live to see a trial. That is why I suggest you stop asking me questions I can't answer. And this is not just about me. Imagine what it would be like if they went after someone close to you. Your family. Your friends. Do you think it was a coincidence that they got to your buddy? There are no coincidences. Everything happens for a reason. Especially when you're dealing with the people whom you are looking for so desperately."

I turned as white as a sheet. I had not expected all this.

"Boris? Are you talking about Boris?"

"Oh, was that his name? Boris. I guess that's who I meant, yes."

"It is his name."

"Oh, he survived? Well, that's strange. They're usually very professional."

"Who?"

"Haven't we just been through all of this?"

"Listen to me, you pompous bastard, you are going to tell me who ordered Boris's murder. You are going to give me his name, or I'll make sure you don't live to see another day. Do you understand?"

"Yes, boss. So what are you going to do?"

"Don't question what I'm capable of."

"Why don't you just pull out your gun and shoot me in the head right now. Right here. C'mon! Show me that you've got a pair of big hairy balls between those legs of yours. C'mon suit, are you a man or a pussy?"

I leaped across the table and grabbed him by the throat. I felt an urge to strangle him on the spot, but I knew I would not. Not because of my career and not because I did not dare to. Even though this scum is of no use to anyone and does not deserve to breathe the same air we do, it would be crazy for me to screw up my life for him. I let go, sat back in my chair and continued as if nothing had happened.

"I'll find these people. One way or another," I said.

"I'm sure you will. Give them my regards when you meet them."

"You're screwed Kolya. You are in shit so deep that you'll be digging your way out for years to come."

"That might be so. Karma is a bitch."

"Yes, karma is a bitch. And if I find out you played a part in this murder, no matter how small your part may have been, you won't just be facing a bullet, but a fate much worse than that."

"Yeah right. You had your chance, and I still haven't seen what's hiding in your pants. Are we done here?"

"For today, yes. But our next conversation won't be as pleasant."

"I'm counting on it."

I stood up and walked out of the interrogation room. I left the station without interacting with any of the policemen walking towards me. Once outside the station, I turned left and quickly made my way to the park. I sat on the bench and watched how my trembling hands pulled the box of cigarettes from my jacket's pocket. I had to call

Boris before he did something stupid.

The telephone kept ringing, but that did not really come as a surprise. I changed my mind even before I started writing the text message. Our phones are encrypted, but that does not ensure one hundred percent safety. There is always someone, somewhere with the ability to spy on you. Your anonymity is nothing but a fleeting memory the moment you connect to the internet, buy a cell phone, order cable television or pay with a credit card. In the digital world, the classic forms of control have lost their meaning, even though they are still in use. This is mainly true of real criminals who knew how to get off the grid. They were the ones we liked best because they were a real challenge. We called them ghosts because that was what they truly were. They had no Facebook profiles, no email addresses, no cell phones, and no credit cards. They never appeared in the media, and Google searches on them came back with no hits. Ghosts.

I turned off my cell phone. I knew it could still be tracked, so I decided to leave it in the office. I was totally relaxed as I walked into headquarters. I was in no hurry, and I did not give away the slightest hint that anything was wrong. I heard Horvat's voice before I reached my office.

"Rok, come to my office! Now!"

I continued calmly towards my office. Once there I took off my jacket, placed my phone into the desk drawer, took a piece of chewing gum from the same drawer and put it in my mouth. I stood still for a moment, then I turned around, closed the door, turned left and walked down the corridor towards Horvat's office. His door was open as usual. I knocked anyway.

"Ah, Rok, sit down. Please close the door."

I closed the door and sat in one of the two chairs opposite him.

"How did the interrogation go? Did you manage to

drag anything out of him?"

Do you think it was a coincidence that they got your buddy? There are no coincidences. I could not take the risk. I had no idea how far Walter's tentacles reached. I trusted no one.

"He didn't give anything up. Nothing worth reporting, anyway."

"Did you offer him protection?" asked Horvat.

"Of course. At first, it seemed he was interested, but then he turned cold."

"Fuck. So we got nothing. Nolan won't be happy. This was our chance."

"I know. I can try again in a few days' time, maybe he'll …"

"That won't happen. He'll be free tomorrow. I've just received the instructions for his release from the court. There's nothing that we can pin on him."

"What do you mean nothing?! What about the snitch? He said he would testify."

"He's changed his mind. We have nothing."

"What about the photographs? The voice recordings? We were spying on him for over a month!"

"You know that the taps have no court backing. And the photographs only show that the bastard knows how to enjoy himself and that he has good taste in hookers."

"I can't believe it. Sometimes I wonder why we even try."

"Think and wonder as little as possible. You'll have to pull up your socks and plunge in head first. If this case slips through our hands, we're done for. And this is not me imagining a worst-case scenario. We've received a final warning from the very top."

"It's the very top that makes our work impossible. It could all be so simple. But as things stand now, we're letting criminals go. Criminals who don't even bother denying that they're involved in the crimes they're accused of."

"That's the way the system works. It's down to us to perform the best work we can within our capabilities."

"And our best men have to pay the price!"

"Rok, I don't like the tone of your voice, and I certainly don't like the direction you're heading in! You can hardly hold me accountable for what happened to Boris. Can you?"

I was aware I was walking on thin ice, but now I have reached the point of no return. There was no way I would remain silent. I have done it so many times before, but I will not do it this time.

"I'm not sure. You might not have been the one to squeeze the trigger, but you did nothing to protect him."

Horvat turned white, then red and looked as if he was going to explode.

"You ungrateful fuck! The next thing I know you're going to accuse me of being on Walter's payroll!"

"I didn't say that."

"You don't have to; your face clearly shows that that's what you're thinking. Listen to me carefully, I'm only going to say this once. You have me to thank for the fact that you're still breathing fucking Ljubljana air. They wanted to get rid of all four of you, those two and you two. I managed to convince them Boris's murder would be warning enough. I protected you. You and your girlfriend. So don't tell me I don't protect my best men. I always take care of my own. Boris was the sacrificial lamb they demanded. It was either him or you. I had to decide between the two of you. Do you understand? So don't be such an ungrateful fucker and most of all don't stick your nose into things you can't handle! You'll see what it's like if you're ever put in my position. The Earth isn't flat Rok, and life isn't fucking Disneyland."

I was at a loss for words. I felt like Icarus must have, the moment his wings started to melt. I should have listened to my father and never join the police force.

"Can I leave now?" I said after a few seconds of silence.

"I guess I don't have to tell you what the consequences will be if you mention our conversation to anyone."

I stood up and looked at him with disbelief for a few moments.

"You are an immoral man, Simon. I trusted you."

"You still can. I told you I always look after my men."

"Not now, nor will I ever be one of your men."

"Are you sure about that?"

At that moment I felt like I knew nothing. I could not trust anybody. Nothing would ever be the same. I had no recollection of how I reached the pavement outside the headquarters. I did not even notice that it was raining. I looked towards the sky and let the raindrops that were sliding down my face mix with my tears. Who am I? Who are the people I have allowed into my life? Life is not Disneyland. Not anymore. My life had suddenly become a runaway rollercoaster. And I am sitting in the front row waiting for us to derail and get splattered across the gray concrete below. Goddamn amusement parks. I never liked them.

CHAPTER NINETEEN

I was sitting in my car in front of Boris's house, slightly intoxicated. The house appeared to be empty, but I decided to wait for a while, even though it seemed highly unlikely I would find him here. Tina had told me he was staying at one of the Ljubljana hotels, but she did not know which one. I bet it was Mons, seeing as that was where we often hid our protected witnesses, but he might as well gone off-the-grid using another hotel as his safe house.

I did not have a plan. After downing a few whiskeys, driving to Dolgi Most and waiting for Boris seemed like a good idea at the time. And here I was, sitting in my car.

My thoughts were violently disturbed by somebody knocking on the passenger's window. I twitched, looked to the right and saw a uniform I recognized. I opened the window.

"Good afternoon, sir. May I ask what you're doing here?"

"Good afternoon to you, officer. I'm on a stakeout."

I showed him my badge. He took it into his hand and glanced at it.

"Wait here."

He marched to the police car that was parked a few meters behind. I had not noticed it earlier. I watched him in the rearview mirror. The two police officers were checking my badge. This was all standard procedure, nothing unusual. Then I noticed that somebody was sitting in the back seat. He had a hood over his head, so I could not see his face. One of the officers turned back to talk to him. The mysterious man nodded. The officer that had taken my badge stepped out of the car and started walking towards my car. He looked around and then leaned in through the window.

"Would you please step over there with me, sir."

"What seems to be the problem?"

"There's no problem, we just need to clarify something, detective Kopitar. Please come with me, and I promise you everything will be fine. We're on your side."

If only I knew what side that was, I thought. I no longer trusted anyone and I most certainly did not trust unidentified police officers and people with hoods over their heads. However, I did not really have a choice. If they wanted to get rid of me, that is precisely what they would do. I could start up my car and try to escape. But I did not. Instead, I opened the door, stepped out of the car and followed the officer. As we approached the car, I began to recognize the facial features of the man sitting in the back. The police officer opened the back door, and I sat next to him. For a while, we sat in silence, looking at each other. I nodded at the officer, but he indicated with his hand that I should remain calm.

"They are on our side," Boris finally said.

"To be honest, I'm not sure which side is ours."

"I can imagine. I was a bit confused at the beginning too."

"So you know about Horvat?"

"I've known for a while."

"And you didn't tell me?"

"I didn't want to put you in danger. Sometimes ignorance is bliss."

"I thought we were best friends. Partners."

"We are. That's exactly why I didn't tell you."

"Listen, Boris … You have no idea how sorry I am that I couldn't do anything to prevent what happened to you and Milena. If I could turn back time, I would …"

"I'll stop you right there before you sound even more pathetic. Sara explained everything. I'm sorry that I lost it. I had to let off some steam. It was all building up inside me. I'm sure you understand."

"Of course I do."

"Great. I'm glad to hear it. Do you trust me?"

"I'm not entirely sure."

"Who told you that your ex was getting it on with a coworker?"

"Umm, you did."

"Who took you in, when you had nowhere else to go?"

"You did that too."

"Have I ever steered you wrong?"

"Never."

"See. It's no different this time. But I need you to trust me completely. And I also need your diary. I've got to know what I can expect. I have to know the future."

"That diary's nothing but trouble!"

"That might've been true up until now, but from now on we're going to use it to our advantage. It's going to be our secret weapon."

"Against who?"

"Against anyone who dares to stand in our way."

"I'm not sure about this, Boris. This shit goes too deep. This case is way over our heads."

"Listen, I need you to back me up one hundred percent! This is not a joke. They'll come after you, trust me. They'll come after Sara, they'll come after your father, your brother …"

"Matej lives in London."

"And you think he's safe over there? Nobody's safe, do you understand? They'll get your family. One by one, until you're the last one left. They'll toy with you, and when they're fed up, they'll kill you. Do you think it's a

119

coincidence that I'm still alive? Do you think they were careless? There are no coincidences. Not in their world. Everything happens for a reason."

There are no coincidences. Everything happens for a reason. I had heard the same words earlier that day during my interrogation with Kolya.

"Kolya said those exact words. Are you one of them? And you're trying to convince me to trust you. It would be better if you just got rid of me straight away!"

"Calm down, Rok. Everything is okay. I'm going to tell you something now, but remember, it's top secret, and it could endanger our entire operation if anyone else hears about it. Are you ready?"

I nodded. After the day I had had nothing could come as a surprise to me.

"There's no Walter."

"Say that again?!"

"Walter's a set-up. We made him up in order to flush out the bad cops."

"But Kolya is working for Walter, we were talking about him earlier today. He almost confessed."

"No, Kolya is one of our men."

I could not move my body. I was sitting there, motionless, processing the information I had just received. Right when I thought that my day could not get any stranger, this happens. I felt as if I was opening up a set of Russian nesting dolls. Each one that I opened revealed another one that was even more fascinating. Causing the previous figurine to vanish from my mind immediately; it became a mere shell. But with some persistence, I am likely to reach the core, the very last doll that cannot be opened. I might like it, or I might think it is utterly ridiculous. Nevertheless, it is what it is. But something remains. You have reached the end. The million dollar question is whether I had reached the last doll or if this one would open too.

"Are you okay, Rok?"

Boris's voice brought me back.

"Yes. I'm not sure. It's been a bit too much of everything to process for one day."

"I can imagine. Go home and sleep on it. I'll get back to you soon. Unfortunately, I can't show myself. They're still watching me, but I promise we'll meet soon."

"Who's watching you? If Walter doesn't exist ... I don't understand."

"Bad people."

"Horvat?"

"Horvat's a small fish, but he's a part of the story."

"He told me today that I have him to thank for the fact that I'm still alive."

"He was telling you the truth."

"But you're alive too. And you said that they don't make mistakes."

"It's true. They allowed me to live because they still need me. They killed Milena because they were confident that I'd try to avenge her, and they were hoping I'd give up our little group in the process."

"Who's in this group?"

"A handful of carefully picked individuals."

"Is Nolan one of them?"

"Yes."

"Tina?"

"Tina doesn't know anything."

"Who else?"

"You know enough for now. Go home, Rok. You're safe, both of you are. We're also keeping an eye on Sara, so you've got nothing to worry about. I'll see you soon, but in the meantime, you need to monitor your diary and share any intel that might be useful to us. We need to be one step ahead of them the entire time. Good luck, pal."

A minute later I was back in my car. Once more, I ran through the entire day in my mind. I tried to find details that could be included in a new reality, a reality that seemed to be changing from one moment to the next. I tried to come to terms with this new reality, which had turned the world that I knew upside down. I undertook an attempt to understand that I had been living in an imaginary world, in an illusion. I realized that nothing would ever be as it was. I thought of Sara. What if she was not who she said she was? I shook my head, trying to put an end to this line of thought. I need to go home. I turned the key and started the engine. I could still see the police car in my rearview mirror. I slowly drove towards home and hoped that this parallel reality, which I embodied, had no more surprises in store for me. What a day.

CHAPTER TWENTY

Six fifteen. I was sitting on the sofa, pouring some Irish courage in the form of a burning golden liquid down my throat. After two glasses of Jameson, I dared to check whether there were any new entries in the diary. I had not told Sara anything, even though, while driving home, I decided that I trusted her completely. When she asked me what my day was like, I chose to reply with the classic "okay." I figured that it would be better if she did not know what was going on. Mainly because I had a hard time understanding it myself and could not explain it even if my life depended on it. I opened the diary and immediately noticed that it included a new entry. I started reading.

April 3, 2015, 6.45
After a few days in hiding, Boris met up with me yesterday and explained everything that had been puzzling me. I'm assuming you've also spoken to him. So I won't give you a detailed report on the conversation. If by some weird chance you haven't talked to him, let me tell you this. Operation Orion Pax is a charade. It was created to flush out corrupt cops. Nolan is clean. He is also one of the initiators of the operation so you can trust him. Don't trust the others. Horvat is immersed neck-deep in this, he didn't even try to hide his involvement during our conversation. Kolya is a mole, but he is on our side. Walter does not exist. Boris and Milena's murders were ordered from within. I have no idea who ordered the killings, neither does Boris, but he firmly believes he was left alive for a reason. Do not discuss this with anyone. As soon as I discover anything new, I will let you know.

I was relieved. I had been convinced that our lives had drifted too far apart on the day that I had fought with Boris. But this was not where the entry ended. There was more at the bottom of the page.

10.35

Kolya is dead. The official explanation is that he slit his wrists after breakfast and bled to death before the policeman found him. I know he was killed, but what I don't know is whether they managed to squeeze anything out of him. Be extremely careful and don't ever try to change what has happened or what will happen! The consequences of that would be too dire, and I would no longer be able to help you. Let life run its course, and I will warn you about any obstacles on the way. Good luck!

I needed another drink. This was getting serious. For the first time since I laid eyes on the diary, I had the power to change things for the better. I can not undo what I screwed up with Boris, but I could save somebody else's life. The temptation was huge. I felt a surge of energy running through my body, energy that I had never felt before. Do I dare to play God? I took a sip. What is the purpose of the diary if I am not allowed to change anything? The outcome would be too severe. The only consequence, which I could see, was that I had the chance to save the life of an innocent man. The world of the other Rok might become different from my world, where Kolya would still be alive, but this should not influence our lives too much. Neither one of us had a significant relationship with him. In my understanding of parallel lives, nothing drastic should happen if Kolya was still alive tomorrow. After another sip of whiskey, I finally made up my mind. Tomorrow morning I will become the architect of my own destiny, no matter what happens.

"Hey, can you help me move the cupboard? Something

fell behind it."

I had forgotten entirely that Sara was at home.

"Of course," I replied. "What've you lost?"

"A book. I bought it today, and I really want to start reading it. Just move it a little so that I can reach it with my hand."

I grabbed hold of the cupboard with both hands and moved it a few centimeters.

"Is that enough?"

"Yes. Great. I've got it. Thank you, sweetie."

A glass of white wine was waiting for her on the coffee table. She sat on the couch, opened the book and started reading. I admired her. I am sure she read at least five books a month. She really loved crime novels, but she also read other books. Occasionally I would suggest one to her, even though I did not read half as much as her. I was probably closer to five books a year. We had a lot of books at home, most of which were stacked on the bookshelves in the study, though some were resting on the various shelves in the living room.

"What's on the menu today?" I asked her.

"The girl on the train."

"That's new."

"Yes, I bought it today at that new bookstore. They just got it in this week."

We were regular visitors of bookshops in town. As a rule, we would only buy books in English because they were much cheaper than books translated into Slovene. Sara loved Matt Haig, while I was more of a science fiction kind of guy.

"Is it a crime story?"

"Yes."

"It's been a long time since I've read a good crime story."

"It's been a long time since you read anything."

"That's not true. I just finished that one, what was it ...

The Ocean at the End of the Lane, by Gaiman."

"That was in December."

"No way!"

"It's true, we were in Bled. Do you remember? Mid-December."

"I can't believe it. How time flies."

"Too fast."

"I won't disturb you anymore. Enjoy your book."

"You're not disturbing me. Is there anything new in the diary?"

"There is, but nothing extraordinary," I lied. "Tomorrow should be a normal day."

"Finally," she said before becoming wholly engulfed in an imaginary literary universe.

CHAPTER TWENTY-ONE

Seven-fifty-five. I stepped into the police station on Trdinova, with a court order in my hand. I knew the judge, so it was not that difficult to convince her about its necessity. I was not lying. Kolya's life was hanging by a thread, and that was precisely what I told her. I left out the details even though I was almost one hundred percent sure she could be trusted. I assured her that we would transfer him to a safe location and emphasized that Kolya was of great importance to the Interpol operation. She handed me a signed and stamped piece of paper without questioning me once, and that was it. The first part of the plan was behind me.

"Good morning," I greeted the officer on duty.

"Oh, Rok! What are you doing here so early?"

"I came to fetch a package."

In detective jargon, a package was a suspect who needed to be relocated.

"Special delivery?"

He laughed at his bright reflection.

"Airmail," I responded.

"O-la-la. Come in, Green is just making coffee."

I stepped into the police station. I could smell the fantastic aroma of freshly made coffee. I walked to Chief Grohar's office and knocked on his door.

"Come in."

I opened the door and stepped in.

"Good morning chief."

"Good morning Rok. What's new?"

"I came to pick up a package."

"Kolya?"

"Yes."

"Well, that was quick. I thought you'd pick him up around lunchtime, but you're here now, and it's only, what is it … eight? You must really be in a hurry."

"We are. Here's my warrant."

I shoved the paper right in his face. He took it into his hands and started reading.

"Everything seems to be in order. Do you want to take him straight away or do you have time for a coffee?"

"I'll take him straight away if that's okay with you."

"Of course it is. I'm used to people from headquarters always being in a hurry."

"That's the nature of the job."

"Come with me. I'll take you to his cell."

"Thank you."

Kolya was lying on the bed, solving crosswords. The sound of the doors unlocking did not seem to disturb him.

"Kolya, today is your lucky day," said chief Grohar.

He slowly put down the magazine and sat up straight on the edge of the bed.

"Oh, Mister Kopitar! Have you come for the second round?"

"I have, but there'll be a slight change of venue. The court has decided you are to be relocated to a top security prison until the interrogation."

He looked at me and raised his left eyebrow.

"It isn't April Fool's Day, so don't mess with me. I'm free, aren't I?"

"You'll be free when I say so."

"I know my rights. If there's nothing you can hang me for, …"

"Interesting choice of words."

"Where are you taking me?"

"I can't disclose you that."

"Kolya, stop talking," Grohar butted in. "Your personal belongings will be waiting for you with the officer on duty. Rok, if I'm no longer needed here, I'll return to my work."

"That'll be all chief. Thank you."

Grohar marched towards his office. At that moment I realized that my plan had worked. I looked down the corridor to make sure nobody was listening. There was not a living soul in sight. The coffee break had done its trick. However, I continued with the show seeing as you never know where a camera or a bug might have been planted.

"I told you that you're done."

"I have no idea what you're talking about. You have no clue what's really happening do you?"

"I do. I'm well aware of it. We've caught a criminal and now we're going to put him behind bars. That's how it's done in a law-abiding state."

"Law-abiding state? This country is knee deep in shit. All of the tractors in the world couldn't even pull it out."

"That might be true, but I believe in our state."

"Then you're nothing but an idiot!"

"Idiot or not, you're coming with me."

"You're playing with fire, suit."

"But you're the one who's going to get burnt if you don't pack your crosswords and come with me immediately."

"Where are we going?"

"I still can't tell you."

He stared into my eyes as if he was trying to read my mind. We stared at each other motionlessly for a few seconds and then he withdrew his gaze.

"Okay, I'll play this stupid game of yours. I'll be out in a few days anyway. You won't get anything out of me because I have nothing to tell. I'm an honest citizen just like you, and that's it. Do you understand me?"

He picked up the magazine and opened it.

"I just want to finish this last crossword puzzle. I'm missing one word. A plea for help. Ten letters. It ends in -cation."

"Invocation."

"Great. I might've underestimated you. I'm ready. Let's go."

We stopped at the officer on duty and collected his belongings – wallet, cell phone, keys, ring, two VIP football match tickets, a box of Marlboro cigarettes, and a lighter. I signed the release papers while Kolya was checking his wallet to see if anything was missing. Then the two of us left the station. I walked straight towards my car, which was parked a few meters from the entrance.

"Hey! Let me have a cigarette before we go. Honestly, that's the least you can do."

I stepped up to him and snatched the pack of cigarettes from his hands. Then I indicated with my hand that he should give me all of his belongings. He immediately understood what I wanted and handed me everything without saying a word. I crossed the road, walked up to the nearest trash can and filled it with the opulent contents, which were guaranteed to make the first scavenging beggar or garbage man, working in this area, very happy. The risk was too high; nothing could be left to chance. Listening bugs and tracking devices are so small and superior these days that even experts can not find them. I used a simple rule. If you are not one hundred percent sure that nobody is listening in or following you, just assume that they are and behave accordingly. Of course, in practice, this means that you have to be on the lookout continually, be careful of what you say, who you are speaking to and remain aware of your surroundings. And especially now, almost everyone is on the grid and only a few clicks away from revealing their private or professional life. Kolya was waiting for me outside the police station. He could have escaped; he had every opportunity to do so, but he waited for me. This made me believe he trusted me and that I could carry out my plan as I had devised it.

"Here, have a cigarette," I said while offering him one.
"Thank you."
"Come, let's take a walk. Let's grab a coffee over there."
"Uff, I would kill for a cup of coffee."
Kolya's life was still hanging by a thread, and now I was involved as well. The plan was simple. I knew that we were quite safe as long as we were out in public. Sure, occasionally someone would be taken care of in the middle of Ljubljana, but I knew all the tricks that they used.
"This will be fine," I said as we walked towards the television station. "Sit down, I'll go in and order. What sort of coffee do you want?"
"A double espresso."
"You've got it."

I ordered the coffee at the bar because I wanted to watch the waiter make it. It is hard to imagine how many murders are committed with poison. Some poisons work instantaneously. Consequently, the target will collapse in the middle of the café or restaurant. It usually looks like an epileptic seizure or a sudden cardiac arrest. However, most poisons work with a delay. There is no effect for a few hours after a person drank the coffee, juice, beer, or any other liquid substance, for that matter, when all of the sudden they collapse and die in the comfort of their own home. Some poisons disintegrate soon after death, which makes them almost impossible to detect.
"A double espresso and a long single, please."
"I'll bring them out."
"Don't worry, I'll wait."
"As you wish sir."

The waiter was about twenty years old. He did not look like a professional killer, but none of them do. It is wrong to assume that hitmen are introverted loners who only manage to have a relationship with their weapons. Sometimes this is true, but I know quite a few of them who are family men with regular jobs. I even knew somebody who wrote invoices for his services. He was self-employed, and he registered his activity as a cleaning service. He was a professional assassin who would kill people for a living and give the state what he owed in the form of taxes and social security contributions. Real life is much more exciting than any storyline we can possibly imagine.

I returned to the table with two coffees. Kolya was sitting calmly in his chair, but his face revealed that he was trying hard to figure out what was going on. He had no idea how much I knew, but he knew that the situation was more severe than he could have ever imagined when he had opened his eyes this morning.

"You're not taking me to prison are you?"

I looked around. Three women were sitting two tables away from us, discussing their boss. The waiter was still behind the bar, passing the time playing with his cell phone. An elderly man with a dog walked by, stopped at the fence that bordered on the garden of the bar for a few seconds, and then continued on his way. The coast appeared to be clear.

I leaned towards Kolya.

"I'm taking you somewhere safe. I'm not sure where to, just yet."

"Why?"

"Well let's put it this way. If I didn't come to fetch you this morning, I would've …"

I looked at my watch which I had decided to wear today.

"… received a message that you slit your wrists in your cell in an hour's time."

He looked at me in disbelief and then poured the sugar from the little sachet into the cup of coffee with trembling hands.

"Don't drink that," I told him.

"Why?"

"Because I said so."

"How …"

"How did I know you'd be killed?"

I was speaking quietly, but I soon realized that the women sitting a few tables away had gone silent and were listening in on our conversation. I turned towards them.

"Is the coffee any good?"

"Excuse me?" the boldest one in the group replied.

"I was just wondering whether your coffee was any good."

"The usual."

"Are you on your lunch break?" I continued the conversation.

"We are on a coffee break."

"Where do you work?"

"At the radio station."

"Do you like it?"

"You know how it is. There are some positive things and some negative ones. But overall it's okay."

"Did you find our conversation interesting?"

"Excuse me?! We weren't listening to you," the other one showed her bravado.

"C'mon. It's not nice to lie at your age."

"This is too much," the third one joined in. "Who are you, mister?"

"That's not important. How long does your coffee break last?"

"That's none of your business," the first one returned to the conversation. "Have we paid girls? I've had enough of this crap."

The first one went towards the bar to settle the bill, while the other two got up and started walking towards the radio station.

"You should learn some manners," one of them shouted at me when they were a few steps away.

"I enjoyed talking to you too," I yelled back at her.

People from the neighboring bar started looking at us. Naturally, we had attracted quite a bit of attention. It was time to change locations. I threw back my coffee, slightly burning my throat, and stood up.

"C'mon. Let's go."

"Where to?"

"The less you know, the better."

We stood up and walked away from the police station on Trdinova, turned left at the end of the building and walked down Kolodvorska Street towards the train station.

"Hey! Didn't you park your car in front of the police station?"

"What did I tell you about questions?"

In front of the Slovene Railway building, we turned left, crossed the street and went straight towards Bavarski Dvor.

"No fucking way! We're going to go on the run using public transport!"

I pulled out a cell phone, that I had bought at the gas station early in the morning, from my pocket. I dialed the number of a taxi driver whom I knew through and through. He said that he would pick us up in seven minutes.

"Do you want a burek?" I asked Kolya.

"At nine o'clock in the morning?!"

"It is never too early for a pizza burek."

"You're crazy."

"Suit yourself."

I stepped to the window and ordered a pizza burek and some yogurt.

While I was eating, Kolya was nervously walking up and down, looking around, and up at the windows of the Telekom building, as if he was expecting a sniper to be hiding somewhere, waiting for the order to send a bullet through his head or heart.

"Calm down. All snipers have taken a syndicate trip to Gardaland."

The way he looked at me revealed his lack of enthusiasm for my jokes.

"How can you be so calm?" he asked me.

"It comes with age."

"You're crazy."

"That's the best foundation you can have for a full life."

Just as I swallowed the last bite, a taxi driver with a face I knew well stopped nearby. I waved at him and indicated to Kolya that it was time to go. He followed me silently to the car and we both sat in the back of the car, each entering from our own side.

"Hi, Meho."

"Good morning Rok. How are we doing today?"

"You know. Same old, same old. Saving lives."

"Better saving them than cutting them short. Where do you want to go today?"

"To Vrhovci."

"To the place you go to die?"

"Exactly."

"Is this some sort of joke again?!" Kolya butted in.

Meho had already turned the taxi around and was driving towards the destination.

"I think you're aware by now that I'm one of the few people you can trust," I said calmly. "I'm taking you to a safe place. You'll spend a few days there, just until this shit calms down."

"In a retirement home?!"

"Have you ever heard of anyone dying from anything but natural causes in a retirement home?"

"I haven't got a clue. I don't have a subscription to Retirement Weekly."

"You'll be in good hands. In the meantime, I'll get to the end of this charade."

"So you know about me?"

"Yes, I've heard you have dual citizenship."

Dual citizenship. An expression we used for somebody who played a double game. Usually, they were mole agents.

"What's going to happen now?"

"You are going on a holiday, while the big boys will finish off this game."

He relaxed in his seat, and his face clearly showed that he was relieved. He had performed his task well and the remuneration, if only he survived to see the end of the story, was ensured. He just might live to experience Cuba. I closed my eyes for a few moments and imagined I was lying under a palm tree on the sun-heated white sand, drinking rum and smoking a cigar. Who would not want a life like that? But people are masochists, and we sell ourselves to whoever gives us the highest monthly wages, which, for most, is barely enough to scrape by through the month. Some are lucky, and they actually do what they always wanted to. The remaining ninety-nine percent do things that they do not care about, for people they do not like, with co-workers whom they hate. Living in an apartment, which they can not afford, socializing with people they do not know, and forsaking to do the things that would bring them joy and pleasure in their spare time. They say that they are so scared of death, but in reality, they are afraid to live. If they are happy, there is something wrong with them. Happiness never lasts, so it is better to never even try. Suffering is what keeps them alive. Any addiction is problematic, but dependence on pain is most characteristic of modern humans. Homo Cruciatus.

Man torturing himself.

CHAPTER TWENTY-TWO

As soon as I sorted out Kolya's new temporary accommodations, Meho took me back to the center and dropped me off at the police headquarters. This might have seemed a misguided idea at first glance, but I had to pretend that nothing unusual was going on. While I was still outside, thoughts flashing through my mind, a familiar voice came from behind me.

"Rok! Where've you been?"

I slowly turned around.

"Oh, Tina. How are you?"

"I'm fine. How about you? Horvat's mad as hell. He's been looking for you since this morning. Apparently, you're not answering your phone."

"I must've forgotten it at the office. What's up?"

"I don't know. He didn't want to tell me, but it seems to be serious. Are you in trouble?"

"It certainly seems so. I have no idea what has gotten into him this time."

"If I were you I would rush up to him and clear it all up. I haven't seen him this mad in ages."

"Thanks, Tina. I'll go to his office right away."

"Smart move."

I took the stairs to the third floor and slowly walked down the corridor towards Horvat's office. Those who kept the doors to their offices open looked at me as if I was a prisoner on death row, taking my last few steps. But I did not feel like a prisoner. I walked with my head held high, steady steps one after the other, and with a smug grin on my face. I knew that nothing could happen to me. I was confident that I would not be sitting down on an electric chair after concluding my short walk. Some might prefer sitting on that disheartening chair to confronting Horvat when he is in the worst possible mood, but not me.

I knocked and opened the door.

"Kopitar! Fucking hell! Come in!"

He rarely called me by my surname. It was clear as day that he was pissed off.

"I heard you've been looking for me?"

"Sit down!"

I did as I was told.

"Do you think this is the Wild West?! Do you think you're a fucking Sheriff? Do you think you can walk around holding cells and set prisoners free without my permission?"

"I guess you must be talking about Kolya?"

"Have you set any other criminals free today?"

"Let me think. No, he was the only one."

"Do you think this is a joke? Do you want to be suspended? You're almost there!"

"There's a first time for everything," I said calmly.

"You're not serious. And I don't need people who aren't serious about their jobs. Do you understand me?!"

"I think seriousness is overrated."

"Listen to me nitwit. This is how we're going to do this. I demand to know where you took Kolya. If you tell me immediately, I might reconsider your suspension. Otherwise, you're done. Got it?! I'll make sure you won't even get a job as a fucking traffic warden!"

"Kolya and I had a cup of coffee, and I let him go after we'd had our caffeine fix."

"Is it your duty to set prisoners free?!"

"No. This was a first. And I have to say that I enjoyed

it."

"Another remark like that and you can hand in your fucking badge. Then we'll see if you've got the balls to talk back like that. Have you got any idea about the magnitude of the shitstorm that you've created? Nolan called me and demanded an immediate explanation. Of course, I couldn't explain squat. I had no idea where you were, and there was no way of getting in touch with you since yesterday evening because your phone, which just kept on ringing, was found in your office drawer!"

"I was wondering where I left it."

"Can you please tell me what's gotten into you?"

"I can."

"Fucking enlighten me then!"

"I sacrificed the queen."

"For what?"

"Important information."

"About who?"

"Kolya told me how I can get to Walter."

Horvat's eyes sparkled, and his jaw dropped into his lap when I fed him that line. He needed to come to grips with what he had just heard, and it took him a few seconds to return to the present.

"Are you serious?!"

"I promised him that I'd let him free after I verified the information that he gave me. Well, his information was correct, and I stuck to my end of the bargain."

"Well, well, well. You truly took me by surprise, Rok. I underestimated you. But this time you've truly excelled yourself. The promotion is yours."

"I don't want a promotion. I like my job the way it is."

"You'll be decorated for this one. By the President himself."

"I don't care for decorations."

Horvat stood up from his large leather chair and opened the door of the wooden drinks cabinet. He took out a crystal bottle and two glasses.

"This one is for special occasions. It's costly," he boasted.

"Yamazaki?"

"No. Hakushu. 25 years old."

"A rare drink. And expensive as hell."

"I told you it's for special occasions."

He pushed the glass into my hand.

"To almost closing the case!" he yelled.

I smelled the contents of the glass. I have never had a whiskey with such a unique aroma. I took a sip and simultaneously realized that I had just shot about fifty euros worth of booze down the hatch.

"Damn good whiskey," I said.

"I told you, I take care of my people. You've proven yourself, Rok. You know I don't praise people lightly."

"I told you I'll never be one of your people. Whoever you are."

"I think you've the wrong idea about all this. The world isn't all black and white, it operates on levels you can't even start to imagine."

"Don't underestimate me."

"I'm not. But the world is like a theater. You only see what's happening on stage. But in the background, there's a whole bunch of people who are making sure that the performance runs smoothly. You have to look deeper, and when you get insight into what happens backstage, into the machinery behind the system, you'll never look at it with the same eyes again."

I drank the remaining whiskey and placed the glass on the table.

"So tell me what Kolya said. How do we find Walter?"

I started explaining. I was making up the story as I went along. Even the world's best fiction writers would be in awe of my tale. I gave descriptions of people who did not exist but were involved in an imaginary network that connected criminals on both sides of the Atlantic. He was listening with the same intensity as that of a child, which is paying attention to his mother who is reading him a bedtime story. And that was precisely what I was selling him. A fairy-tale. I offered him a behind the scenes glimpse of an imaginary world, and he was buying it all – word for word. I could see it in his eyes. He did not doubt me for a single moment. But I left the best for last.

"Do you remember the dealer we found with five kilos of cocaine in his apartment about a year ago?"

"Omić?"

"That's the one. Well, we had him, but he got away."

"Omić is Walter?"

"Exactly."

"The guy lives in the center of Ljubljana! I just saw him walking his dog a few days ago."

"You said it. The world's a theater."

"I have to get a search warrant for his house immediately!"

"So you're planning to arrest your boss?"

He immediately became serious.

"I told you last time not to stick your nose where it's not wanted. I'm not who you think I am."

"I know you're damaged goods," I said.

"You know nothing. Life isn't an action movie. The real world isn't divided into good and bad people. There are no heroes and no happy endings. This world is plummeting into oblivion and there's nothing you can do to stop it. Mankind is sailing on a ship that hit an iceberg decades ago. The only question is, when will it finally sink?"

"So you decided that you'd rather be a rat that gets to abandon ship before that happens?"

"No. I decided to join the orchestra and play all the way to the sad ending."

"So I'm the rat? Is that what you're trying to say?"

"You're the lifeboat sailing in the wrong direction.

You're a good man, Rok and you should never forget that. I am who I am. I'm a piece of a huge three-dimensional puzzle, playing my part. Just like you're playing yours."

"It seems we're not part of the same puzzle."

"Oh, but we are. We are part of the same puzzle, passengers on the same ship, actors in the same play. It's only our roles that are different."

"So what's going to happen now?" I asked.

"Nothing. We're going to arrest Omić."

"And release him again?"

"We'll see about that. You know that there are no guarantees in our line of work, unpredictable twists are a part of our walk of life."

"But you have insight into what's happening backstage."

"The backstage that you're referring to has many layers, which are constantly changing. Nobody gets to see the whole picture. Look, I want you to stay on this case. Forget what you think you know. Focus on the fact that we're about to crack an international criminal operation."

"I can't. I'm contaminated. They're watching me," I said.

"All of us are constantly being watched. This has never bothered you before."

"It's different this time around."

"Don't worry. I'll call the cleaners."

"No need. I'll take care of it myself."

"Alright, but don't forget to call Nolan. We need to get the green light from him before we take action."

"Don't worry, I'll call him. Simon, there's just one more thing …"

"What is it?"

"When this is all over, you'll have my badge on your desk."

"What are you saying?"

"Some boats are destined to sink."

CHAPTER TWENTY-THREE

Nolan did not want to discuss the case on the phone. He said that the matter was too sensitive to leave anything to chance. He suggested we meet tomorrow, in person, in Paris. I agreed, and as soon as I hung up, I booked a flight to The City of Light. I have not set foot in those vivid streets in a very long time, but I knew that a change of scenery is what I needed. I felt my stomach growling. Apparently, the burek had been digested.

I took the telephone from my jacket pocket and punched in nine numbers.
"Hello?"
"Hey. How do you feel about an early lunch?"
"Rok? Did you change your number again?"
"Only temporarily. Celica, in fifteen minutes?"
"Twenty. I still need to send off a couple of emails."
"Deal! See you soon."

I opened the drawer and took out my old cell phone. I checked my missed calls. Horvat, Tina, Nolan, Sara, and two unknown numbers. Nothing unusual. I placed it on the table and put my car keys next to it. I would not need either until next week. I stood up and left the office. I was desperate for a dose of nicotine. Cigarettes help me with clearing my mind. Metelkova was a ten-minute walk away. Sara was a regular at Celica, which did not come as a surprise to me seeing as she worked at the Ministry of Culture just across the road. I was not a regular patron at this restaurant. I was only there once every two months. The food was excellent and the service was quick, but it was at Metelkova. A place that I frequented way too often on duty for it to still appeal to me in my spare time.

When I arrived, I saw that Sara had already made herself comfortable in the garden. I stepped into the former prison building, turned left, passed the reception desk and stepped through the glass door into the summer garden. Sara noticed me and waved. I sat on the orange plastic chair opposite her.

"Tough day?" she wondered.

"One of those when I ask myself why I do the things I do."

"That bad?"

The waiter stopped at our table.

"Oh, Miss Sara. You've brought your boyfriend today?"

"Well, apparently, he has to eat too."

"Have you decided what you're having?"

I gazed quickly at their daily lunch menus.

"I'll have the risotto," said Sara.

"Bring me the trout."

"What would you like to drink?"

"I'll just have some water. But I assume Rok will have something stronger."

"I'll have a glass of white wine."

The waiter nodded and rushed towards the kitchen.

"I'm going to Paris tomorrow. I have a meeting with Interpol."

"Aren't you the lucky one. Are you staying just for the day?"

"I'll be back on Sunday night."

"Great. You haven't been to Paris since time immemorial have you?"

"Uff, ten, no, nine years."

"That's a long time. I envy you. It's gorgeous this time

of the year when everything is blooming."

"I'm not sure I'll have the time to appreciate nature's splendor."

"I know, but try to recharge your batteries a bit."

"I know I should. I've had some wild days."

The waiter brought the food.

"You'll tell me everything in the evening. If you decide to, of course."

I nodded and focused on the trout. We spent the next few minutes in silence, fixed on the food in front of us and on the thoughts in our minds. There was a storm brewing in my head. I was used to sudden turnarounds, it was a part of the job description, but what had happened over the past ten days was a bit too much, even for me. I had become a part of a broader story, which I did not understand, and I was eaten up by this Chinese arithmetic. I had never been so tired in my life.

"Rok, are you okay?"

I looked towards Sara.

"Yes. No, I don't know. I can't wait for this to end."

"I can imagine. Is there anything I can do to help you?"

"I'm thinking about resigning."

"I can totally understand that. You should do what you feel is right. I'll stand by you no matter what you decide and no matter what you'll be doing in life."

I gave her a little smile. I was looking at this person sitting opposite me, wondering what I had ever done to deserve such a beautiful soul in my life. She was so understanding and overflowing with love. I had never felt so loved before. I had never felt so alive before. I had been an iceberg until she came and turned me into a river.

* * *

April 4, 6.45 am
I'm sitting in a cafe at Brnik airport, thinking about an important step in my life. I'd always wanted to be a detective, I dreamt of becoming one as a child, and now I'm contemplating turning the ship around and set sail for calmer waters. I know you are facing the same dilemma, but let me honestly tell you that the decision is, in fact, quite simple. We'll become fathers by the end of the year. With a woman who's ideal for us. Do you remember how, years ago, when we broke up with Martina, we swore we'd never give up our dreams for a woman? Of course you do. Well, now our aspirations have changed. They've become a burden that's pulling us into life's dark abyss, a nightmare. A story that we both believed in collapsed like a house of cards. We no longer know who we work for, or who we're up against. If there has ever been a time to turn over a new leaf and start anew, it would be now. What do you think?

I leaned backward, crossed my hands behind my head and stared into the void. His thoughts were the same as mine. There was no other way. He was right. Our dreams have changed. If I had once believed naively that my work saved innocent people from dangerous criminals, it had now swung round and changed over the past few days. I no longer knew who I could trust, who I worked for and who I was saving from whom. It was time to hit the brakes and try to stop this runaway train so that I can get off. A part of me wanted to get to the bottom of what is going on, discover the identity of the train driver and be there when the train reaches its destination. But there was also the other, irrational part of me. The one that came to life, after global warming popped up, in the form of Sara. In the past, I would have given anything to have the chance of coming down hard on an international criminal organization, regardless of the cost. But today, the stakes seemed too high. It was time to say goodbye to my childhood.

* * *

"I've thought about it, and I've reached a decision. I'll hand in my notice on Monday."

"Smart choice. Over the past few days, I've noticed that work was weighing you down. Well, more than usual."

"The main problem is that I can't see the whole picture anymore. It used to be simple. We were the good guys, and we were after the bad guys. Now I can't tell the difference. I don't know who's who anymore."

"I can understand that."

"And then there was all that stuff with Boris. At first, I thought that he was done for, but recently it's been revealed to me that he plays a vital part in this entire story. Nothing is as it used to be."

"Have you met up with Boris?" Sara asked.

"Yes, he told me you spoke to him. He told me you explained a few things."

"He visited me at work a few days ago. He said I can trust him completely and that I shouldn't mention our meeting to anyone, not even you. He told me that he'll find you."

"He did find me. I do feel that I can trust him. Even though nothing would really come as a surprise to me now."

"Boris has been your friend ever since you were kids. If there's anyone you can trust, it has to be him. I know you're full of doubts, but try to relax."

"I can't."

"You only need to pull through this weekend and then it'll all be over."

"It's never truly over. Not in this business."

"I'm looking forward to walk down this path with you."

"You're too good to me."

"That's far from the truth. You're underestimating

yourself again."

"I'm only telling the truth. What have I ever done to deserve you?"

"Being who you are. I've never met a man who's more honest than you. You're not perfect, nobody is. But I love you with all my heart. You complete me, and you make me feel secure. You never try to limit me in any way. I always wanted a man like you by my side. I'm not too good for you, I'm exactly what you need. And you're what I need."

I was left speechless. But words were unnecessary anyway. I leaned towards Sara and kissed her. A few moments later, we were tearing each other's clothes off, reveling in an endless ocean of passion. The sun had set, and it was dark outside. A full moon was shining proudly in the center of the pitch black sky. If I could have stopped time, I would have at that very moment. It was so damn perfect that I wanted to pinch myself to make sure I was not dreaming. But I did not. There are some dreams you never want to wake up from.

CHAPTER TWENTY-FOUR

I was trying to unwind at the airport café, sipping coffee. I had one more hour before takeoff. I would be in Paris around nine-thirty, and the meeting with Nolan was scheduled for midday. He had not told me where the meeting was going to be held, but that was not unusual. The matter was too delicate, so any breach of security was unthinkable. I had packed lightly, seeing as I was only going to stay in Paris for one night. Two pairs of underpants, two pairs of socks, three T-shirts, a jacket, an umbrella and that was it. I also brought my laptop, but only because of the diary. As soon as I connected it to the airport Wi-Fi, I checked for a new entry, but there was none. I shut it down and put it back into my bag. I swallowed the last drops of my coffee and set off towards the check-in counter. This time, I had to check in my luggage because my suitcase contained my service gun. Otherwise, I would have taken it all on board with me as carry-on luggage. Once I got past the security check, I moved towards gate number one where the plane was already waiting. A few minutes later, the doors opened, and we boarded the plane. The flight was peaceful and nothing to write home about. Nobody was sitting next to me, and there were approximately fifty passengers on the airplane. After we had landed, I waited for my suitcase and set off towards the exit. Once outside, I lit a cigarette and observed how the taxi drivers were circling a herd of weary travelers like vultures. One of them waved at me and started walking towards me.

"Monsieur Kopitar?"

"Yes."

"Come with me."

"Can I finish my cigarette?"

"Of course, we're not in a hurry."

Once I put out the cigarette, I followed the stranger to the car. It looked like an ordinary taxi, but I knew it was not. I put the suitcase into the trunk and sat on the back seat. Jean-Pierre, if the identification card on the dashboard was to be believed, drove away.

"Is that your real name? Jean-Pierre."

"Oui."

"Where are we going?"

"To the hotel."

"How long have you been working for Interpol?"

"A bit more than two years."

"How do you like it?"

"It's a mixed blessing."

"Just like any business."

The next few minutes in the cab were marked by an unmistakable deafening silence. It was apparent that Jean-Pierre was not a talkative guy and that was fine by me. However, in the end, it was him who broke the silence.

"Slovene, eh? I've never been to Slovenia. Is it nice?"

"Yes, it's nice. A small country, friendly people, wonderful nature."

"I might come over during the summer. Do you have a seaside?"

"We do."

"The sea rocks."

Silence reigned once again. Jean-Pierre turned on the radio. Our drive to the hotel was accompanied by modern French beats.

"We've arrived," said Jean-Pierre just before he stopped the car.

I looked through the window. The name Prince de Galles stood proudly on the jutting roof. I had never heard of it, but it seemed extremely posh.

"Are you sure this is the right hotel? I was expecting something less luxurious."

"This is it. Mister Nolan will be waiting for you in the bar at midday."

I looked at my watch. Ten-fifteen. I had enough time to take a shower and grab a coffee. I wanted to call Sara and tell her I arrived safely, but it was too dangerous. I headed towards reception instead.

"Hello," I greeted the receptionist. "I hope I'm at the right hotel."

She took my passport.

"Welcome to our hotel Monsieur Kopitar! We've prepared room 210 for you. It is on the second floor. The lifts are over there, and somebody will be here shortly to help with your luggage. Alfonse! Alfonse!"

"There's no need, thank you. I'm sure I can manage on my own."

"As you wish, sir."

I took the elevator to the second floor. My room was on the right side of the hall. I swiped the card through the slot and opened the door. I stepped into a hallway where I first noticed a coffee machine. The hall led to a room that I would identify as a reception room. Continuing down the corridor, I reached another door, behind which was the bedroom. It was a standard sized hotel room. There was another door in the bedroom, and this one led – as I expected – into a large bathroom, covered in wood and marble. I took my clothes off and stepped into the shower cabin. I turned the water on and enjoyed the steady stream flowing onto my skin.

* * *

"I'm truly grateful for your contribution to our operation. I'm sorry you are leaving us," said Nolan after I passed over all the information I had gathered over the past few days and explained to him that I was bringing my career, as a detective, to an end.

"All good things have to come to an end eventually," I replied.

"Would you like to come and work for us in London? We could do with a man like you."

"Thank you for the generous offer, but I'll have to reject it. It wouldn't be right. I'm not the right man for you."

"I seriously doubt that. After what I've seen and heard you are precisely what we need in our department."

"Thank you for the compliment. But my decision is final."

"I respect that. But how will you cope with civilian life?"

"I haven't got a clue, but I won't know until I try. I do have a feeling that I'll manage one way or the other."

"Okay. Then all I can do is wish you the best of luck on your new path."

He stood up and put out his hand to shake mine, as a token of his respect and as a solemn goodbye. His grip was firm and determined, entirely in line with his character. Then he turned around and left. That was it. No fireworks, no drum roll. Life is not a movie festival. Nobody rolls out a red carpet in front of you or places a small statue in your hand just because you made the right decision. There is no applause, no victory speech. No limousine to take you down a new path surrounded by a screaming horde of fans. Nobody is going to write articles about you. There will be no footage of you broadcasted on national television. Life happens in a place where nobody is physically present. In our minds and our hearts.

* * *

In the evening, after soaking up the Parisian scenery, I returned to the hotel. I had walked through a good part of the center, tried a few excellent French wines and had escargots for lunch – they did not disappoint me, but they also did not thrill me.

"Bonsoir, monsieur Kopitar," I was greeted by the receptionist.

"Bonsoir," I replied.

"Somebody called you."

"Did they leave a name or telephone number?"

"Unfortunately not. But they did leave a message."

"What was the message?"

"Quod incepimus conficiemus."

"I don't understand."

"It's Latin. It means, what we have started, we will finish."

"What the hell is that supposed to mean?"

"I don't know, monsieur. That was all he said."

I stepped into the room. There was a mini bar on the right, under the coffee machine. I opened it and saw that it contained an unopened bottle of Jameson. I took it from the fridge, opened it and took an honest swig from it. Then I moved to the living room and sat on the couch. What we have started, we will finish. I opened the bag and took my laptop out. Maybe I will find an explanation for what is going on in the diary. I took another sip of whiskey while my computer was booting. I clicked on the document and scrolled down to the last entry.

Rok, I hope you see this in time to do something about it. There was nothing I could do. Sara is dead.

I felt a sudden pain in my chest. It felt as if an elephant was sitting on it. I started shaking uncontrollably, and everything went dark. After a few moments, my vision returned, and I could continue reading.

She was killed in our house, at precisely 20.05. Somebody shot her in the living room, four times. It seems as if she knew the killer seeing that there was no sign of forced entry. The patrol that was in front of the house acted immediately, but they were too late. The killer escaped, and there was nothing they could do to help Sara. This is my last entry. My life has lost all meaning and will end soon. You can still change the past. Good luck!

I checked the time. It was seven forty-five. I had twenty minutes. I instinctively reached for my cell phone, but I immediately realized I had not brought it with me. I looked around. I saw the landline phone to my left. I grabbed the receiver and typed in Sara's number. No reply. I tried again. I was unsuccessful. Again, and again. "The number you have dialed is currently not available. Please try again later." I could not lose any more time. I called headquarters.

"Crime investigation. How may I help you?"

"Detective Kopitar speaking. I request an immediate intervention at number five, Cimperman Street."

"Who did you say was calling?"

"Kopitar, badge number one-one-eight-seven-four-five-one-eight."

"One moment please."

"I haven't got the time for this. A murder is about to take place!"

"One moment, sir."

It took approximately thirty seconds before I heard a familiar voice on the other side of the line.

"Rok?"

"Simon! There's no time to lose. Something is going to happen to Sara!"

"Are you drunk?"

"Listen, I've never asked you for anything, please just do me this favor without asking any questions."

"Where are you?"

"In Paris. What's that got to do with it?!"

"Okay. Calm down, everything is fine. I'll drive there myself and make sure nothing happens to her."

"Thank you."

"It's my pleasure. What we've started, we'll finish."

"What did you just say? Hello? Hello?! Simon!"

We were cut off. Suddenly I was overcome by anxiety. What had I done?! I called Sara again. I had to warn her. The number was still unavailable. Police! I typed in the number of the police station on Trdinova.

"Police. What's your emergency?"

"Detective Kopitar speaking. I need an urgent intervention on number five, Cimperman Street. It's a matter of life and death!"

"One moment sir."

"I don't have a fucking moment! Somebody is going to get killed!"

"Calm down sir. Where are you located?"

"It doesn't matter where I am. Send patrols to Prule, now!"

"One moment please."

I heard voices in the background. They were talking about me. Somebody mentioned Horvat.

"Horvat's crooked, listen to me! Don't listen to him, send a patrol there!"

"Everything is under control, sir. A patrol car is on its way."

"You're not listening to me! Horvat's a crooked cop, he's the perpetrator!"

"Calm down detective. The situation is under control. Everything is going to be taken care of. Good night."

"Hello? Hello!"

I sat on the sofa with the handset in my hands. It slowly slid from my hand. My eyes filled with tears. I stepped to the suitcase and took the gun from it.

Fourteen minutes. Fourteen fucking minutes to go and there is nothing I can do. And God knows I tried, I really did. I did everything in my power to prevent it. I feel so small. Insignificant. A speck of dust in this vast mysterious Universe. I am going to lose the love of my life, and I am just sitting here, downing a bottle of Jameson, trying to keep my tears from flowing. I am about to end my pathetic life with my service Glock. I can not and do not want to live without her.

Twelve minutes to go. Seven hundred and twenty heartbeats. I will have to make the most of them. But will this change anything? No. Life is not a fairy-tale. There are no happy endings. That is just some bullshit that the movie industry tries to sell us. An illusion of reality. All stories end in tears. I would like to crack open the skull of the jackass who said that every new beginning is disguised as a painful ending, and eat his fucking pea-sized brain. Ten minutes. One hundred breaths.

I took my Swiss Army knife from the suitcase, opened up the blade and tested its tip with my finger. I placed my left hand on the table and shoved the knife through it, using my right hand. No hesitation, whatsoever. The small knife dug itself into the wood. There was hardly any blood. No pain. As I was looking at the red handle of the blade that had pierced my palm, I felt a tingling sensation in my index finger.

Seven minutes. One hundred and thirty people will die of starvation. The world is neither beautiful nor fair. If God exists, he is either deranged or he has a terrible sense of humor. Sara gave purpose to my life. She made life bearable. For a while, I even believed that the world made sense. I should be grateful for the beautiful moments that we got to spend together, and for everything that she has given me. Instead, I am furious that fate would play such a cruel trick on me. It gave me the perfect woman, only to snatch her away from me less than a year down the line. I honestly believed that there was something I could do about this. At one point, I felt strong enough and assumed that everything would work out. I knew exactly how it would play out, but in the end, there was nothing I could have done differently to change the outcome. Even if I had changed certain things, it would start all over again eventually, heading towards a predetermined goal.

There is so much knowledge transferred through wires, and through the air. However, the final result is always the same. Nothing changes for the better. The human race is corrupt. We can turn the world into a planet of prosperity and spiritual growth, but instead, we are doing the exact opposite. We are holding onto anger, intolerance, and hatred. We use the technology developed by the military-industrial complex to widen the gap between the rich and poor. We are beyond saving. The only solution to save our planet is to eradicate humankind. Once the people are gone, natural order will be restored.

The time has come. The gun appears to be lighter than usual. In fact, I do not feel its weight at all. They say that your entire life flashes before your eyes when you die. I hope that only the last eight months of my life will flash before my eyes. I have to choose a good memory. The most beautiful one. I am going to leave this planet thinking of the most wonderful woman in the history of mankind, with a smile on my lips. Strange, I never noticed before that the trigger is a bit rough. I hear a telephone ringing in the distance, followed by a loud bang.

EPILOGUE

"Nobody's answering."

"Try again."

"Still nothing."

A motionless body was laying in the middle of the living room. Two policemen were leaning over it.

"He's dead," said the first one.

"He always seemed to be such an honest guy. And now this," added the second.

"The other guy was imprisoned until yesterday, and today he's a hero."

"I know, who would've thought?"

Sara stepped out onto the terrace and gazed at the full moon.

"Are you also looking at it?" she asked the night sky.

A male figure walked up behind her and held her shoulders.

"Did Rok ever tell you what he thought about the Moon?"

"No."

"Ask him when he comes back home."

"I will, Boris. Thank you for coming."

"You have that man over there to thank for."

He pointed to the living room where a man, unknown to Sara, was giving a statement to the policeman.

"Who's that?"

"Someone whose life Rok has saved. And now he saved yours."

"It's just like in the movies."

"Exactly, but this time it has a happy ending."
"Did Rok tell you he's going to resign?"
"No."
"Paris is his last hurdle as a detective."
"What's he going to do now?"
"What he loves most. He's going to live."

If you're reading this, you've reached the end of the story.

If you liked it, please rate it on Amazon and Goodreads.

If you didn't like it, you can rate it anyway.

You can find me on:

Twitter: @jaka_tomc
Facebook: /tomcjaka

info@jakatomc.com

https://jakatomc.com

Printed in Great Britain
by Amazon

53120246R00099